Swallowcliffe Hall

Grace's Story

1914

Books by Jennie Walters:

The Swallowcliffe Hall *series:*

Downstairs:
Polly's Story, 1890
Grace's Story, 1914
Isobel's Story, 1939
Upstairs:
Eugenie's Story, 1893

For teens:
See You in my Dreams

www.jenniewalters.com

Swallowcliffe Hall

Grace's Story

1914

Jennie Walters

Half Moon Press
London

Author's Note

I am very grateful to Chris Baker, both for his wonderfully informative website about World War One, 'The Long, Long Trail', at www.1914-1918.net, and for his checking of my manuscript to make sure it was historically accurate. Thanks also to Philip Kirk for letting me read his grandfather's First World War diary, to Julian Fellowes for the bus anecdote, and to Venetia Gosling and Harriet Stallibrass for their helpful suggestions about the end of the story.

First published in Great Britain in 2006 by Simon and Schuster UK under the title *Standing in the Shadows*
Whilst we have tried to ensure the accuracy of this book, the author or publishers cannot be held responsible for any errors or omissions found therein.

ISBN-10: 149127283X
ISBN-13: 978-1491272831

Cover design by Amanda Lillywhite, www.crazypanda.com
Cover photograph of Edna Rauh, now Mrs Edna Rauh Millican, reproduced by her permission; with thanks to her and Mrs Susan Kane
Other cover photographs copyright © Jennie Walters, 2011

Chapter One

This day will be momentous in the history of all time. Last evening Germany sent a curt refusal to the demand of this country that she, like France, should respect the neutrality of Belgium. Thereupon the British Ambassador was handed his passports, and a state of war was formally declared by this country.

From *The Times*, 5 August 1914

'OH GRACIE, YOU ARE A SIGHT,' my mother said, picking leaves out of my hair. 'I hope none of the family saw you like this.'

We're almost the same height now, so her brown eyes were looking straight into mine. You can tell we're mother and daughter, I suppose, although my hair's a little fairer than hers, but it has to be said that light brown hair and dark brown eyes are about the only two things we have in common.

'Now sit down while I put the kettle on,' she said, 'and tell me all the news from the Hall. Are you getting on any better in the kitchen?'

I tried to ignore that question. 'Two footmen and one of the garden lads have volunteered for the army already. Alf told Florrie all about it.'

Florrie's first kitchenmaid above me at Swallowcliffe and Alf's her young man - he works in the gardens too. Florrie thought it wouldn't be long before he joined up, although he had an elderly mother who wanted to keep him wrapped up in cotton wool and we knew she wouldn't let him go in a hurry.

'You don't say.' A shadow passed across my mother's face and she shook her head a little, as if to clear it. Then she pulled out a chair opposite me. 'Now, who was that I saw coming back from the railway station in His Lordship's Rolls-Royce? Noisy great thing, it is! And the way that French chauffeur or whatever they call him sounds the horn, you'd think Judgement Day had come.'

My parents live in the gate lodge at Swallowcliffe Hall. I moved out as soon as I started working in the big house and now I share a room up there with Florrie and Dora, the scullerymaid. Ma used to be a housemaid at Swallowcliffe, but once she married my father (who was a footman at the time), of course she had to give that up. She loves the place as much as ever, though, and opening the gates lets her keep an eye on all the comings and goings. Whenever I call in at home on my afternoons off, I get a regular grilling about what the Vye family are up to.

'They're having a big luncheon out on the terrace,' I told her. 'It must have been the Duke and Duchess of Clarebourne you saw in the Rolls - they've come down from London specially. And old Lady Vye's there, of course.' (She's Lord Vye's widowed mother, and quite a battle-axe; I call her the Dragon Lady to myself. The way she can look at a person sometimes, it's a wonder flames don't come shooting out of her mouth.)

'Oh, lovely,' Ma sighed. 'I bet the table looks a picture. Now, what did Mrs Jeakes give them to eat?'

'Cold beef and chicken, veal-and-ham pies, and a whole poached salmon. Almond cheesecake and plum tart to follow.'

I had an idea what might be coming next. Sure enough, my mother pounced. 'What did you make? Have you moved on to pastry yet? Surely you can't still be on vegetables and garnishes?'

'I tried my hand at mayonnaise this morning,' I offered, hoping this would satisfy her. (Of course the wretched thing had curdled, but Ma didn't need to know that.)

The look came over her face that I'd come to dread: half disappointment, half worry. 'You ought to be moving on, Grace, getting your foot on the ladder,' she said for the twentieth time. 'Everyone knows Alf's only waiting for a place as head gardener and a house along with it before he asks Florrie to marry him. There's a real chance for you to become first kitchenmaid if you work at it.'

But how could I get excited about that? Most of the time all I wanted was to tear off my apron and run out of the kitchen as fast as my legs could carry me. Sometimes when I was standing over the stove in my thick stockings and heavy apron, the dress underneath plastered against my body like a hot poultice, it felt as though I was suffocating. There wasn't even a window at head height to give us a breath of air; they're all set up high in the wall so we couldn't waste our time staring out. You can imagine what that was like - as if the whole room was one big oven and Mrs Jeakes, Florrie and I were being roasted inside it. I kept thinking some giant was going to reach down through the window and pluck me out when I was done.

There was no point trying to explain, though. I knew exactly what Ma would say. 'Count yourself lucky! In my day, the second kitchenmaid had to be up at half past five every morning to light the range, and woe betide her if it wouldn't draw. You've got it easy with that gas stove, not to mention hot water at the flick of a tap. The number of times I had to traipse up and down stairs, filling and emptying those blessed hip baths!'

The trouble is, no matter how much she might grumble about the old days, she still thinks working at Swallowcliffe Hall is the be-all and end-all of everything. And I'm not sure that it is, for me. So I tried to change the subject. 'What's going to happen, Ma? What will they do at the Hall if all the lads enlist?'

It wasn't only the young men at Swallowcliffe who'd been on my mind. Ever since we'd heard that war had been declared with Germany, I'd been worrying about my older brother, Tom. As luck would have it, he'd just turned nineteen so he wouldn't even have to lie to the recruiting officers about his age. He'd followed in my father's footsteps (Da being coachman at the Hall, running the stables and driving the carriages) and was working as a groom in Suffolk for the Ildersley family. There's four years between the two of us, but I'm closer to him than either of my sisters even though he's a boy. Perhaps it's because I'm so much of a tomboy myself, as Ma keeps pointing out.

I couldn't bring myself to say Tom's name, but surely she must have been thinking about him too. Why were we chatting about motor-cars and luncheon parties as though everything was the same as usual?

'All the lads *won't* enlist,' my mother declared over the shriek of the kettle. 'We'll teach the Kaiser a lesson and the whole thing will have blown over by Christmas, you'll see. Oh, bother it!' She had managed to splash boiling water over her hand and would have dropped the teapot if I hadn't been there to rescue it.

'Here, I should be doing this,' I said, sitting her back down in the chair and wishing I could have bitten off my tongue. Just because someone doesn't mention a thing straight out, doesn't mean it's not on her mind.

We chatted about this and that while we drank our tea; safe, everyday gossip that had nothing to do with the war or my prospects in the kitchen. And then we both caught the clip-clop of horses' hooves outside - quite a few of them, from the sound of it - so I went to the front window to see whether the gates needed opening.

'Ma? Come and look at this!'

It was such an unexpected sight that I couldn't trust my own eyes. Together we watched as a line of horses came walking up from Stone Martin village, one after another, not saddled or bridled but tied by their halters to a long rope which kept them together. Some I recognised: a pair of huge Shires with feathery fetlocks who pulled the hay carts at harvest time, two bays from the dairy who collected butter and milk from the farms, and my favourite, the butcher's black mare following on behind them. I'd christened her Raven when I was little (though I once heard Mr Ryman call her Bessie) and used to bring her apples when Tom and I had been scrumping. She'd come trotting over to the fence to meet me, and delicately twitch the apple from my hand with her soft whiskery lips like a genteel old lady.

An army man, dressed in khaki, slapped her on the rump and shouted something to make her get along. What could be happening to all these horses? Where were they going? Not to the Hall, that was all we knew; they were being driven straight past our gates. I hurried outside to find out, my mother close behind.

'They're being shipped across the Channel,' the soldier told us. 'Off to serve their King and country - not that they've any choice in the matter.'

'But how will we manage without them?' I protested. 'You can't just take them away!'

'Oh yes, we can, young lady. The government says so and we've paid their owners fair and square. What do you think our boys will do without horses to bring them supplies and drag the guns about?'

I knew Mr Ryman thought the world of his fine mare; he'd brush her coat till it shone like black satin and always got out of the cart to lead her up the steep hill on the other side of Stonemartin. He wouldn't willingly have let her go for a hundred pounds, especially not if there was a chance she'd be hurt. 'Good luck, Raven. Keep safe,' I said, stroking her warm, smooth neck and wondering if I would ever see her again.

There was nothing more we could do. Ma and I had to stand there and watch that long line of horses disappear down the road: all of them patient, steady creatures who were known and loved in the village. A gang of children had come running along at the end of the procession and several of the little ones were crying. There were tears in my eyes too. It didn't seem right, sending animals across the sea to a war which men had started.

'Let us through, would you? We're expected,' called a loud voice. We turned around to see two more soldiers, these ones riding horses of their own and looking like officers, waiting at the gates which my mother - careful as ever - had closed behind her.

'Oh my heavens, they're going up to the Hall too. Of course!' she gasped, a hand flying up to her mouth. 'I wonder if your father knows about this? He never said a word.'

'We have to warn him!' I didn't know which way to turn, everything was so sudden and unexpected. It hadn't occurred to me to think how I could reach the stables before two men on horseback; nor, more to the point, what was to be done once I got there.

Ma still had her wits about her. 'Take Tom's bicycle from the shed. I'll give them a drink and keep them here as long as I can. Hurry, Grace!'

I hitched up my skirts and set off hell for leather down the drive, my hair whipping out behind me and my head in a whirl. Those soldiers couldn't take the Swallowcliffe horses too, could they? It would break my father's heart.

'There's nothing to be done, Grace. We have to let these men do their job.'

Father was busy sweeping the yard; a chore for Bill the stable boy, by rights, though he didn't seem to be around.

'And what about *your* job? Are you just going to stand there and wave goodbye to that too?'

Sweep, sweep, sweep, my father went - like some machine. What was the matter with him? Didn't he realise what was happening? But then he stopped and looked at me for a second, and I saw the pain in his eyes. 'How can it be different for us up here than it is for everyone in the village? We can't go on driving carriages about in front of people who've lost their working animals. They've done their duty and now we have to do ours.' He went back to his broom.

'Do all of them have to go?' I could hardly bring myself to ask.

'The ponies can stay, and Daffodil. She's too old to be of much use - probably wouldn't even survive the crossing. They've let us keep Her Ladyship's hunter for now, and Moonlight to pull the gig. The others are off to Southampton.'

And then to war: the words hung in the air between us.

'I'm sorry, Da.'

He nodded, and now I understood why he couldn't look me in the face.

I propped Tom's bicycle against a wall and went into the stable block: my favourite place in the whole of Swallowcliffe Hall, for all its crystal chandeliers and fine paintings. It has a high vaulted ceiling held up by marble pillars, flagstones underfoot with a drainage channel down the middle, and a row of stalls, each with its own hay manger and name plate. The stables felt particularly cool and airy that day after the glare of the sun, and little puddles of water lay on the floor from a recent washing. The smell was as sweet as ever: fresh straw, saddle soap and warm animal bodies all mixed up together.

I started walking along the stalls to take a last look at so many old friends. Major and Rocket, Dolly and Bramble, who pulled the larger carriages; Pearl and Snowflake, two greys who could make a gig or phaeton fly along like the wind; Mercury and Gemini, kept for hacking out and hunting; gentle Rosa, for the novices to ride. I had to give each of them a kiss for luck, and by the time I got to Rosa there was such an ache of sadness in my throat, I could hardly breathe. When I laid my cheek against her side, she bent her head down to mine and nuzzled my hair as if to comfort me. Her breath felt warm on the back of my neck, like a blessing.

I couldn't bear to leave her - and then, about to go, I suddenly caught sight of a tall chestnut horse in the stall opposite. Surely not? It couldn't be!

A shadow flickered across the light; I turned to

see my father framed in the doorway, broom in hand. 'Not Copenhagen too?' I asked him. 'He wasn't on the list, was he?'

Da shrugged. 'His Lordship told me to bring him in and keep him with the others. He says they're bound to want a fine creature like that - some general will probably take him for riding about on parades.'

'But Copenhagen's not ours to send away. He belongs to the Colonel! Does he know about this?'

Colonel Vye is His Lordship's younger brother - Master Rory, as my mother speaks of him in a forgetful moment (His Lordship is Master Edward, would you believe, which sounds even more unlikely). He lived in London and kept his horse stabled up there for most of the year, but he'd take him to the Hall every summer to stretch his legs and have a holiday in the countryside with some fresh grass to eat. The Colonel wasn't at Swallowcliffe that afternoon; I'd heard Mr Fenton, the butler, telling Mrs Jeakes that he wouldn't be down from London to join the party until the evening. 'Busy at the War Office, apparently,' and you could tell just being able to say that made Mr Fenton feel important too. Colonel Vye used to belong to the Household Cavalry but had to leave when he was wounded in the Boer War, although he can still ride. He'd brought Copenhagen to Swallowcliffe as a colt, ten years before, so that my father could help break him in over one long summer.

'I knew that one would be something special from the moment I clapped eyes on him,' Da was fond of saying. 'He seems to know what to do before you've even thought of telling him.'

Perhaps that's why they named him Copenhagen, after the Duke of Wellington's favourite horse. I rode him myself once, when I was no more than six: Colonel Vye put me up on his back and I took him round the yard to show Her Ladyship how steady he was. (Ma had a fit of the vapours when she found out, although I was never worried for a second.) Lady Vye loves riding, but His Lordship - well, that's a different story. He had a terrible hunting accident when he was a young man which nearly killed him and never got up on a horse again. The stables at Swallowcliffe would probably have been full of motor-cars if he'd had his way, but with the rest of his family thinking just the opposite, I suppose he had to grit his teeth.

'This isn't right!' I said. 'We can't let them take Copenhagen, not before he has to go.'

My father shrugged. 'I've had my orders; His Lordship was quite clear about the matter. Now run along. They'll be here in a minute and I don't want you getting in the way.'

I'm not sure exactly when the idea came into my head; as I walked over to Copenhagen's stall, it felt as though my body were obeying instructions from somebody else. I lowered the bar and slipped inside. 'Come on, boy,' I whispered, quickly attaching a lead rope to his halter and taking him out.

'What on earth d'you think you're up to?' My father was too astonished to do anything other than stare at me, for the moment.

'Say he broke out of the field, or you couldn't catch him, or he's cast a shoe. Anything you like,' I said, hurrying past him on my way to the mounting block. All that mattered was to get Copenhagen out of there before the army men arrived. There was no time to bother with a saddle or bridle, but I'd ridden bareback on the Swallowcliffe ponies plenty of times as a child, and this was a horse I trusted to behave himself - even though he was a fair size. Hitching up my skirts, I grasped a handful of chestnut mane alongside the halter rope, hauled myself on to his back and teetered there for a moment with my bottom waggling in the air. Not particularly dignified (lucky there was no one but Da to see), but Copenhagen stood as still as a statue, thank goodness, until I managed to swing a leg over and straighten myself up. The ground looked a very long way down.

'Grace, you come back here right now!' Father had broken out of his trance and was running towards me, but he was too late; I squeezed my heels against Copenhagen's side and we were off! I heard Da shout again, caught a glimpse of his pale, upturned face, then we were out of the stables and away, clattering over the cobblestones into bright sunshine. If Lord Vye and the soldiers had been in my way, what on earth would I have done? Ridden straight past them, I suppose, for my blood was up and I wouldn't have stopped for the Kaiser himself - but luckily the yard was empty. Copenhagen blew down his nose, scenting freedom at last after a day shut up in the stables, while I jolted about on his back like a sack of potatoes.

I didn't dare turn around to see if anyone was watching as we careered out of the yard, miles of open parkland ahead of us and the east face of the Hall behind, but it felt as though a hundred pairs of eyes were boring into my back. Any second now, someone was bound to glance out of one of those tall windows. The last thing they'd expect to see was a kitchenmaid making off with the Colonel's horse, riding astride with her skirts and petticoats tucked up into the bargain! The very thought of it made me laugh out loud, and Copenhagen twitched his ears back and forth as though he were sharing the joke. We charged down a path which led away from the house and through a gate out into the park. Copenhagen set his head towards a wooded slope half a mile or so away, which would be the perfect place to hide until the soldiers had gone. A stretch of open grassland lay ahead of us and he eased into a canter; such a smooth, rolling gait that it felt like sitting on a rocking horse, and a relief after the bumpy trot. Clamping my legs against his sides, I buried my hands in his mane and held on to the coarse, slippery hair for dear life. A thrill of excitement ran through my veins. We'd done it! We had given the army the slip - this time, anyway.

We were nearly at the woods by now, but the horse showed no signs of slowing down. I began to feel afraid. Surely he couldn't keep going at this pace? 'Hold on,' I called. 'Not so fast!' The trees were looming up in front of us; I could see a path of sorts among them, but it was overgrown and tangled. 'Wait!' I shouted again, more urgently this time, as we plunged into the coppice and hurtled along the track. Brambles tore at my clothes and twigs were snapping all around me. 'Stop,' I begged, throwing myself low around the horse's neck as we crashed through the undergrowth. 'Please, stop now!'

After what seemed an age, at last I felt him lurch back into a trot. I straightened up to see what lay ahead - and that's when it happened. In one split second, a branch had loomed up across the path in front of me; ducking down to avoid it, I lost my balance and felt myself falling, the world spinning around me in a sickening whirl of sky, leaves and tree trunks. Then came a bone-jarring thud. After that, nothing more except darkness, and pain.

Chapter Two

*Everywhere along the country road one meets horses, by twos
and threes, dozens and scores, being brought into the temporary
depots where they are to be taken over by the various units,
packed into the waiting trains and despatched to the scene of
action.*

From *Country Life,* 15 August 1914

I HADN'T BEEN KNOCKED UNCONSCIOUS, only
winded. Gradually my head cleared and I found
myself lying on my back by the side of the path,
staring up through the canopy of leaves to a patch of
blue sky, far above. It seemed too much of an effort
even to raise my head, but I had to find out where
Copenhagen was. Shakily I propped myself up on
my elbows and glanced around. He was standing a
little further up the path, looking back at me with his
head down low and a sheepish expression in his eye.
All very well playing the hang-dog now, I thought.

16

Then we both became aware of a noise that made me, at least, feel quite alone and helpless. Someone was running down the track towards us. I could hear feet pounding on the ground, branches cracking and a loud whirring of wings as a bird somewhere flew up in alarm. A young man in cricket whites came rushing round the corner, sending Copenhagen backing into the undergrowth with a snort of fear.

'Easy, boy,' he said, slowing down and approaching the horse with his hand outstretched so as not to frighten him any more. 'There, now. No one's going to hurt you.' He reached for the trailing rope and tied it over a branch, patting Copenhagen's neck and talking to him all the time in the same quiet, calm voice. Then he turned to me. 'Are you all right? Have you broken anything?'

'I don't think so.' I tried to arrange myself in a more dignified position, but the effort made my head swim and suddenly I felt violently ill.

'Here, put your head between your knees.' He was beside me in an instant, his hand pressing down on my back, forcing my head towards my legs. It was horrible.

'Don't! Let me be.' I pushed his arm away, fighting for breath. I couldn't disgrace myself in front of him; that would be the end.

'Sorry. I thought it would help.'

My eyes were shut but I could sense him rustling

around in the leaves next to me. What was he doing now? Why didn't he just go away and leave me to die in peace? Then I felt something soft around my shoulders and he was leaning me gently back until I came to rest against ... a tree trunk, it must have been. That was better. I sat there until gradually the whirling in my stomach settled to a flutter and stars stopped dancing in the darkness behind my eyelids. I opened them. There was the boy, sitting against another tree a few feet away, watching me. I closed them again.

Neither of us said anything for some minutes; the silence thundered in my ears, but I wasn't up to breaking it. We sat and listened to the birds singing, and Copenhagen nosing about in the undergrowth. When I looked again, the boy was still watching me. He had untidy fair hair falling on to his forehead and grey-green eyes, I happened to notice, the same shade as the bark of the elm trees around us. His cricket sweater was the soft thing at my neck; it smelt of dried grass and Sunlight soap.

'So, Grace,' he said, smiling. 'Nice afternoon for a ride.'

He might have thought that was funny, but I didn't. And however did he know my name? 'That's Uncle Rory's horse, isn't it?' he went on. 'I recognise the white star on his forehead.'

All at once everything fell into place. I would have to be sprawled over the path in front of Philip

Hathaway, one of the family. (Whatever would my mother have said? I could only hope she never got to hear of it.) Philip is the son of Lord Vye's younger sister - known to Ma in absent-minded moments as Miss Harriet, which is the most ridiculous of all, since she's been married to a doctor for years and looks decidedly matronly. The Hathaways live not far from the Hall. Philip's a year or so younger than my brother Tom, and at one time the two of them were the best of friends - before they grew old enough for people to notice. They'd spend hours together in the stables when Philip came over to Swallowcliffe to learn how to ride, getting up to all sorts of mischief. 'Go away, Grace!' I can still hear them telling me. 'Girls aren't allowed.' It must have been eight years or more since then, and three or four since I'd last seen him. I had always been a little jealous of Philip for taking my brother away, and I didn't like him a great deal better now.

Still, something had to be said. 'I'm sorry, Master Philip - sir. I didn't realise it was you.'

'Come on, you don't need to "sir" me. There's no one to hear; they're all at the cricket.'

Of course, I remembered now. There was a big match on that afternoon: His Lordship's team against the servants'. So that's why Bill wasn't sweeping the stable yard: he was a demon spin bowler. 'Shouldn't you get back there?' I asked.

Philip shook his head. 'I'm batting last. They

won't get around to me for ages yet.' He stretched up his arms, then crossed them behind his head and leaned back. 'Thought I'd take a break. All that talk about whether the French Riviera's going to be ruined for holidays next season, and whether it's more patriotic to go out to parties or stay at home. As if any of that matters!'

Well, I had to agree with him there. 'I know exactly what you mean,' I said, thinking of luncheon parties and curdled mayonnaise.

'Do you?' He looked at me with that smile in his eyes. 'I thought as much. When I saw you galloping up the hill, I said to myself, now there's a girl who can't bear to peel potatoes a minute longer and needs some time on her own to think about things.'

How arrogant he was! I had no business losing my temper, but what with feeling so peculiar and undignified after my fall - and perhaps also because there was no one around to overhear, as he'd pointed out - I just couldn't help it. 'There's no need to make fun of me! Does working in the kitchen mean I haven't the right to an opinion like anyone else?'

'Calm down. I didn't mean it like that,' he said. 'Come on, you have to admit I've a right to be curious. Does Uncle Rory know you've taken to exercising his horse? He probably wouldn't mind if you saddled him up first.'

There was nothing for it: I had to explain. In the end I decided to come out with the truth, since nothing else sprang to mind.

'Weren't you worried about getting caught?' Philip asked when I'd finished the story. 'Anyone could have seen you. And how are you going to get the horse back again?'

'He could easily have broken out of the field and wandered off somewhere. I'll say I came across him in the woods.' Somehow I struggled to my feet, but the dizziness came again and I had to grab hold of a branch to steady myself until it went away.

'Take it gently,' Philip said. 'Here, see if you can walk. There's a good view of the house from where I was sitting, further up the hill. We can watch from there until it's safe to go down.'

He untied the horse and I followed them slowly up the path to reach the point where it skirted the edge of the trees. My stomach hurt with every jarring step I took, but gradually it became easier to get along; Philip found me a fallen branch to use as a walking stick, which helped. We stood there together with Copenhagen and gazed down at the cricket pitch, to one side of the house beside the rose garden, with little figures dressed in white dotted all over it.

'This war is going to change everything,' Philip said, looking at them. 'How can they not see it?'

'Maybe it's time for everything to change.' We're like the pieces in a kaleidoscope, I thought, swirling about when somebody twists it. Who knows what pattern we shall be in when the kaleidoscope comes to rest?

'Well, this is a cosy little scene.' A cold voice cut through the air, making us both whirl around. 'You must excuse me for interrupting.'

It was Colonel Vye. 'I've come to fetch you back to the cricket, Philip,' he said. 'But you clearly have other things on your mind. Perhaps you'd like to tell me what you're doing with my horse?'

I tried to jump in and explain that I was the one who had taken Copenhagen, and why, but the Colonel was having none of it. 'You'd better run along now,' he said. 'I think my nephew can account for himself.'

So that was that: I was dismissed, and had to leave without another word. I stumbled down the hill in a daze of fury and shame, neither knowing nor caring whether they followed on behind. You could see Colonel Vye thought we'd arranged to meet up there in the wood: his precious nephew and some flighty young maid. He probably didn't even recognise me as the coachman's daughter who'd ridden his horse round the yard all those years ago. Yet I'd taken Copenhagen for his sake!

How could I have been so stupid? The soldiers would come back for the horse another day, my father would end up in trouble with His Lordship, and now Philip was having to explain himself to his uncle. Even if he told Colonel Vye the truth, the story would sound so far-fetched no one could possibly believe it. I felt a niggle of guilt about that; but then again, I hadn't asked for Philip's help. Why did he have to get involved in the first place? He'd only made everything worse. I was angry with him, too, besides Colonel Vye - but most of all I was angry with myself.

By the time I'd reached the Hall, this anger had frozen into a kind of icy resolve. I decided not to have anything more to do with the family than was strictly necessary, whatever the circumstances - neither Colonel Vye, nor Philip Hathaway, nor any of them. Philip would just have to get out of this mess as best he could. After a quick wash and change of clothes in our attic room, I flew down the back stairs to start the evening's work. There was to be a special dinner that night, because Mr John Vye, His Lordship's half-brother and the youngest of the old Lord Vye's sons, was off to France the next week, and the family had gathered for the whole weekend to wish him well. Let Mrs Jeakes be in a good mood for once, I prayed, hoping to creep unnoticed into the kitchen. No such luck. She was standing behind the table, sharpening a large carving knife on the whetstone with a face like thunder.

'You're ten minutes late,' she said, not even bothering to look at me. 'Why weren't you here at half past five?' She didn't wait for an answer, which was all to the good as I could hardly tell her the truth and couldn't think of anything else to say. 'There's a roast leg of mutton for dinner. What are we serving with that?'

I racked my brains to try and remember what had been chalked on the slate that morning. 'Parsley sauce?' I certainly like to eat parsley sauce with mutton; Ma cooked it for us once at home and it was delicious, so creamy and fresh alongside the dry old meat.

'Caper sauce, you numbskull!' Mrs Jeakes growled, leaning towards me over the table with the knife still clenched in her fist. Her face was a mottled shade of puce, framed by downy wisps of pale hair at each side which had escaped from her cap. It made me think of a dandelion head that has turned to thistledown and been half blown away by the wind. 'Caper sauce and carrots, so you'd better get cracking.' The words shot out of her mouth like bullets. 'What have you done to your face?'

Even though I was stiff and sore all over (and would probably be black and blue with bruises by the next morning), the only injury you could see was a long red scratch across my cheek; from one of those vicious brambles, most probably. 'I went for a walk in the woods this afternoon and fell over. Sorry, Mrs Jeakes.'

'You went for a walk and fell over.' She stared at me for a few seconds. Then she laid the knife down very deliberately on the table, as though she had to force herself to let it go. 'You are my challenge, Grace Stanbury,' she said quietly. 'You have been sent to test me, and I shan't be found wanting. I am going to turn you into a kitchenmaid if it kills me in the process, which at this rate is highly likely. So you might as well make up your mind to stop shilly-shallying about with your head in the clouds and start pulling yourself together. Now, what do we need for caper sauce?' That low, menacing voice was making my knees tremble; I'd rather she shouted at me.

'Capers, Mrs Jeakes,' I replied faintly.

She nodded her head. 'Go on.'

'And butter.'

She let out her breath. 'Then you'd better go and fetch them, hadn't you? And hurry up!' The last two words were roared out at top volume, which gave me such a shock I nearly fell over backwards. (I noticed Florrie biting her lip not to giggle, which wasn't very kind, but I'd probably have been the same.)

Dinner was served to the family in the dining room at half past seven, and supper in the servants' hall at nine; we kept plates warm for the footmen. You had to keep your wits about you once the meal started. Have you ever seen those jugglers at a fair who spin plates on top of long poles and have to keep dashing from one to another to stop them falling? That's what it felt like to me, scurrying around the kitchen. The hours we'd all spend: chopping and slicing, rolling and pounding, roasting and boiling, from morning till night. Out went the dishes, looking almost too good to eat; back came the dirty plates what seemed like two minutes later to be washed up in the china room so the whole process could start all over again. Meal after meal, day after day - it made you wonder what was the point.

When Dora came through from the servants' hall that evening to tell us they were ready for their bread and cheese, she had some news to pass on. (Luckily, Mrs Jeakes had gone to eat her meal with the rest of the upper servants in the housekeeper's parlour by then, so we were free to gossip.) Poor Dora: she has a terrible stammer and when she really, really wants to say something, it gets worse.

'The C-Colonel's g-g-g …'

'The C-Colonel's g-g-going to F-F-F …'

'Henry h-heard that the C-Colonel m-m-m …'

My ears had pricked up, as you might imagine. All evening, I'd been half-expecting a summons from upstairs to come and account for myself, and the very mention of Colonel Vye's name made me even more nervous. Did he know I worked in the kitchen? Had he complained to Lady Vye about me? You can't hurry Dora, though; any extra pressure and she collapses completely, like a soufflé in a draught.

'Sit down,' Florrie said, pulling out a chair. 'Take a deep breath - there's no rush.'

At last Dora came out with it. 'The C-Colonel's

g-g-going to F-F-F - you know where - !' she said, all in a rush. 'He's j-j-joined up with his old r-r-regiment. He won't be f-f-f-fighting, but he'll be r-r-riding ab-b-bout with m-m-m-messages and r-reports and things.'

So Colonel Vye probably had more important things on his mind. I let out my breath - and then it occurred to me that perhaps he might be able to ride about (as Dora put it) on Copenhagen, and that what I'd done might turn out to be not quite so foolish after all. 'I wonder if they'll let him take his own horse,' I said, fishing for news.

'Oh, Grace! You do come out with the strangest things,' Florrie tutted. 'What does it matter which horse he has? I'm sure they won't expect him to go around on some old mule. It must be a dangerous job, though, and he's not a young man. I hope he'll be all right.'

'At least he d-d-doesn't have a f-f-f-family to w-worry about,' Dora said.

Not like Mr John Vye, with his wife expecting another baby at the end of the year. I knew all about Mr and Mrs John Vye because my sister Hannah works for them as a nurserymaid and loves every minute of it (they live in a big house the other side of Stone Martin village). Hannah's the one in our family who really takes after Ma, although she's shorter and plumpish. A round peg in a round hole, that's Hannah.

Florrie thought it was wonderful that Mr Vye should be fighting for his country. 'He knows where his duty lies,' she told me smartly. 'The war's not going to wait for his convenience. Think how he'd feel if he missed it!'

I could imagine how Mrs Vye would feel - very relieved, most probably - but Florrie seemed to be in the mood for a lecture, so I kept quiet. When Dora had taken through the bread, cheese and chutney for the servants' hall and the family were busy with their treacle tart (an extra large one, as it was Mr Vye's favourite), as well as meringues, strawberries and cream and a blackcurrant ice from the still room, I took off my apron and slipped out of the back door. Mrs Jeakes would be in the housekeeper's room for another half hour, I reckoned; it was time to make peace with my father. He'd be waiting to take the Dragon Lady back to her lair in the dower house after dinner.

Walking into the half-empty stables was very sad. The ponies were still out in the field with the weather being so warm, so only a few of the stalls were occupied. It was quite dark by now, but I could make out Moonlight's pale head over the iron bar (wondering what had happened to his friends, no doubt). And there was Copenhagen - safe and sound, nibbling from the hay rack. I went over to his stall, pleased to see him even though we'd ended up in such trouble.

'Not planning another break-out, are you?' My father's voice made me jump. 'I ought to ban you from these stables, by rights.'

'Sorry, Da,' I turned to face him. How angry was he? It was hard to tell in the gloom. 'I don't know what came over me.'

'Another of your tomfool ideas, that's what came over you,' he grumbled, going into Moonlight's stall with a couple of brushes. 'You're going to end up in serious trouble one of these days, my girl.'

'I won't do anything like that again,' I promised, watching him give the horse a quick going-over.

'You'd better not.' But his voice had softened a little. 'Honestly, Grace, you could have been killed, taking off on a great creature like that without even a saddle or bridle! What were you thinking of? When I saw the Colonel riding him back to the stables I knew you must be lying somewhere with a broken neck. Don't you ever put me through that again.'

My poor father; I hadn't thought how worried he'd be. 'I'm sorry, Da,' I said again. 'Truly, I am.'

'So you should be. His Lordship thinks I went against his word and he doesn't like it. There'll be consequences, you mark my words.' He sighed. 'Well, you can help me get this one ready for the gig. Might as well make yourself useful now you're here.'

I went to fetch Moonlight's trappings from their pegs in the harness-room, where a dim light threw shadows on the wall. Everything was clean and tidy, as usual; Father always keeps the stables shipshape. 'A place for everything and everything in its place,' that's what he likes to say.

We tacked up Moonlight together. He's such a calm, steady horse, and I was so thankful we'd been able to keep him, at least. I backed him between the shafts of the gig while my father watched, his face grave and thoughtful.

When I'd finished, out came the lecture. 'Grace, you and I are both servants in this house,' he said. 'If we're ordered to do something, we have to do it right away and no argument - that's what we're paid for. We can't start deciding what we think about the idea. If Her Ladyship orders beef for dinner, Mrs Jeakes won't serve chicken instead because that's her favourite, will she? You worry me, my girl, you really do. If you carry on this way, I don't know what's going to become of you.'

He went off to fetch his hat while I held Moonlight steady and gazed up at the stars, tiny pinpricks of light in the black velvet sky. What was going to become of me? I didn't know either. The future stretched ahead: a long procession of treacle tarts, caper sauce, mayonnaise and mutton. Was that it?

Chapter Three

You are ordered abroad as a soldier of the King to help our French comrades against the invasion of a common enemy. You have to perform a task which will need your courage, your energy, your patience. Remember that the honour of the British Army depends on your individual conduct.

From *Field-Marshal Lord Kitchener's address to the British troops,* 1914

I HAD MEANT TO GET UP at dawn the next morning to say goodbye to Copenhagen, but after all the excitement of the day before, I slept like the dead until morning. Colonel Vye had gone by dinner time and I'd heard nothing from him, or Philip either, so it looked as though my little adventure would stay a secret between the three of us - and Father. I tried to put it out of my mind and concentrate on my work.

At least things seemed to be going our way in

the war. We servants took to meeting up in the hall together at four o'clock, where Mr Fenton would read us out reports from The Times (His Lordship usually having finished with it by then) over tea and seed cake. Everyone cheered when we heard that our troops had met the Germans at a place in Belgium called Mons, and given them quite a beating with not too many losses on our side.

'There you are,' Florrie whispered. 'I told you Mr Vye had to hurry up or the war would have finished without him.'

After that piece of good news, however, everything went rather flat, and then someone heard a rumour that British casualties had been worse than first thought. The next thing we knew, word came that our soldiers were retreating; the Germans were driving them back into France.

'B-b-but why?' Dora asked when we were back in the kitchen. 'I th-thought we were w-w-winning!'

'Because our boys are outnumbered and there's no one to back them up,' I told her. 'It's not that we're losing, though, so cheer up! They're just finding a better place to dig in and then they'll give those Germans what for.'

The trouble was, we didn't have enough soldiers in our little army, not even alongside the French. The call for more volunteers went up in earnest now; even the picture card in Father's pack of cigarettes was telling him he should be off to war. 'There's a place in the line for you!' read the cheery caption, above a row of men in uniform with one empty space in the middle. I wondered what he thought about that, though I didn't like to ask. He was too old to offer his services, and the head of a family besides, but maybe he still felt he should have been doing something. Everyone seemed to have a son, a brother, a friend or a sweetheart who'd signed up. Lord Vye gathered us all together in the hall one morning to announce that he would understand if any more of the menservants wanted to enlist; he'd give them their old jobs back at the Hall when the war was over.

'These are testing times for everyone.' He looked severely at each of us with his dark, deep-set eyes. 'We shall all have to redouble our efforts, those who stay at home no less than those who travel abroad. "They also serve who only stand and wait," as the poet Milton says. There may be times when you are called upon to perform some small extra task which has not fallen to you in the past. Let there be no complaining! This is a way for you to help your country, and you should be glad of the chance to do so. The humblest scullerymaid can play her part as well as the highest general.' (Dora quivered beside me.) 'Think of our brave soldiers who may be called upon to make the ultimate sacrifice for you, and go about your work willingly on their behalf.'

'He talks so nicely,' Florrie sighed afterwards.

'Do you think he writes it out first?'

By that time - early in September - we were a smaller group already. Isaac and Jim, second coachman and groom, had been quick to leave: they'd signed up with a cavalry regiment the day after the horses were taken away. Our stable lad Bill had wanted to go as well, but apart from being only seventeen, he was too short into the bargain. You needed to be at least five foot three to join the army, and he was only five foot two. At least my father had somebody left to help him, though; there might have been only a few ponies and horses left by now, but they still needed looking after and exercising every day. The stables had to be kept tidy, too, with all the harness cleaned and oiled and the gig spotless, ready for the two Lady Vyes to be taken about.

It's confusing, there being two Lady Vyes. The younger one, His Lordship's wife, is a completely different kettle of fish from her mother-in-law. For a start, she's American and not half so starchy. She remembers all our names - even Dora's - and she'll smile and ask how you are in a way that makes you think she really wants to know. (Of course I always reply, 'Very well, M'lady, thank you for asking,' even if I could drop with tiredness and my feet are killing me.) Ma first met Lady Vye when she visited the Hall as plain Miss Brookfield and says she hasn't changed a bit since then, even though it was twenty-five years ago.

Anyway, young Lady Vye was always going off to Hardingbridge for some sort of committee work to do with the war. And twice a week, twenty or more ladies would arrive at the Hall to take up residence in the drawing room for the afternoon. Florrie and I used to wonder what they were up to: they certainly had a healthy appetite for cake and scones at five o'clock.

'Knitting,' one of the new parlourmaids told us, when she came to collect a plateful of cucumber sandwiches. (All three footmen had gone by then, so the fetching and carrying and waiting at table was done by Mr Fenton and a couple of maids in smart livery. Very hoity-toity they were, too.) 'The ladies are making gloves and socks for our soldiers overseas. And balaclava helmets.'

I don't know why that should have been so funny, but Florrie caught my eye and we both collapsed in fits of giggles. The maid looked down her nose at us but I didn't care; it was such a relief to laugh when everything was really so solemn and sad. That night I lay in bed, staring up at the cracks in our bedroom ceiling and thinking about the changes that had come upon us, seemingly out of the blue. All those young men, leaving the Hall ... I could see a map of Britain in my mind's eye, with black lines of soldiers like marching ants pouring out from every town and city, down to the coast and across the Channel. I wondered about Tom. We hadn't heard from him, but surely he'd soon be volunteering if the country needed men so badly that they were even sailing over to help us from places like Canada and Australia. You could always count on Tom to do the right thing. Of course I thought then that the war would soon be over, like we all did, but the nights began to seem very long and bleak. I'd lie there while worries raced in circles round my head, listening to Florrie's heavy breathing and Dora grinding her teeth as though a rusty spit were turning.

At last I decided to try and work so hard that sleep came the minute I lay down, which wasn't difficult in the current circumstances. We were finding ourselves 'called upon to perform some small extra tasks', as Lord Vye put it, every day - and they weren't particularly small, either. Poor Mr McKinley, the head gardener, was the worst off. Alf had still not volunteered for the army (his mother having begged him on her knees to stay), but the other four garden lads had gone. You could hardly blame Mr McKinley and Alf if the rose beds had begun to look tatty and the raspberries were rotting on their canes with no one to pick them. It was becoming quite a problem, though, because we were running out of vegetables for the dinner parties that were still being held every weekend at the Hall. Lord Vye had gone up to Scotland as usual for the grouse season (as if there wasn't enough shooting going on across the Channel) and come back with a sackful of birds that we had to pluck and serve roast for dinner with pommes de terre Lyonnais and a red-wine gravy. How could we manage that when there were scarcely enough potatoes for five guests, let alone fifteen?

So Mrs Jeakes had a word with Mr McKinley, and the upshot was that Dora and I took to spending an hour or so each morning in the kitchen garden, digging up vegetables and picking fruit. (Mrs Jeakes didn't want Florrie out there, wasting her time making sheep's eyes at Alf.) I didn't mind that at all - anything to be out in the fresh air and away from the cook's eagle eye. The weather was still bright and sunny, but with a freshness about it that lets you know summer's nearly over so you'd better make the most of it. My favourite time of year, probably, although spring is lovely too in its own way. Then one day I had the shock of my life. Who should I find, digging over one of the seed beds in a pair of Da's old boots and her hair tied up with a red spotted handkerchief, but -

'Ma? Whatever are you doing here?'

'What does it look like I'm doing? Taking a bath?' she replied tartly. 'I'm working over this bed so you'll have cabbages and onions for the table next spring.'

Apparently the land agent who ran the estate and employed the outdoor workers, Mr Braithwaite, had put up a notice outside the village hall to ask for help in the Swallowcliffe gardens. Ma had gone to see him without telling any of us, and now she would be there five mornings a week, along with two other ladies from the village. It made sense when you came to think about it (our garden at home was a picture), although I'd never heard of married women coming back into service - that was something new. The money would certainly come in handy, though, and anyone could see Ma was delighted to be working at the Hall again.

'Now I can keep more of an eye on you,' she said to me when she came into the kitchen with the vegetable hamper a couple of hours later. 'Time for a cup of tea and a chat, Mrs Jeakes?' You can probably imagine how I felt about that.

There was one bright spark on the horizon. Our Aunt Lizzie was coming to Hardingbridge, to sing at the Palace Theatre, and she had sent us tickets for five seats - in the gallery, no less. My other sister Ivy couldn't get the evening off (she was a parlourmaid up in London), but Ma and Da, Hannah and I were going, and we'd probably take a neighbour with the spare ticket. There was no point asking Tom: apart from a couple of weeks in the summer, he only ever had the odd day off occasionally and it was too far to come from Suffolk just for one night. But Alf was treating Florrie too, so they'd be joining us. I couldn't wait! We were going to see Aunt Lizzie backstage before the show, and then have supper at a proper restaurant when it was over.

'Eliza Everett', that's my auntie's stage name. You'd never have thought we could have someone so glamorous and exciting in our family; sometimes even I find it hard to believe she could possibly be my mother's little sister. I've seen her perform three times now, and it's always a treat. She'll have the audience in the palm of her hand from the very first song - including Ma, who forgets how much she disapproves of Lizzie and ends up singing along to the old favourites like the rest of us. And when it's time for a ballad, 'Miss Everett can reduce a grown man to tears', just like the billboards say.

I'd been looking forward to that afternoon for days; when at last it came, there was an extra surprise which made me so happy I could have burst. Da and I came home at dinner time to find our kitchen full of chat and laughter, and my brother Tom with his long legs stretched out under the table.

'Look who arrived this morning, without so much as a word of notice!' Ma said, although you could see from the way her eyes were shining that she didn't mind. 'I sent him to tell Mrs Howard she couldn't have her trip to the Palace after all.'

'How's my favourite sister, then?' Tom said, sweeping me up in the air (which is how he greets all three of us).

'Oh, put her down,' Hannah grumbled. 'She's going to bang her head on the ceiling in a minute.'

'How have you got so tall and grown-up, Gracie?' Tom asked. 'They must be feeding you on something special at the Hall these days.'

'Hard work and fresh air,' I replied. 'Hasn't Ma told you? We're gardeners now, on top of everything else.' I hadn't seen my brother since the beginning of the year (he'd gone over to Ireland in the summer to work at the horse fairs), so maybe I had changed a little - but he was just the same. Same wide grin crinkling up his eyes, and same hearty laugh that you can't help but join in with. All the girls like Tom, and it's not just because he's turned out so handsome; he makes you feel as though you're on the brink of an adventure, and that it's going to be fun.

We were off on an adventure that day, and in a very jolly mood as we left for the railway station. I'd had some problems deciding what to wear, but had settled in the end on my navy taffeta skirt (a little too full to be fashionable, but so much easier to walk in) with a pretty white voile blouse that Ivy had sent me from London. It had come from her mistress - who didn't mind handing on her old clothes so long as she didn't have to see the parlourmaid wearing them - and set off my white straw hat quite perfectly. Florrie had leant me her grey linen coat and I felt altogether pleased with myself, strolling along beside Hannah.

She told me the latest news from Mr John Vye, over in France. He'd been fighting near a river about thirty miles outside Paris, to try and save the city from being invaded. Apparently they'd managed to hold off the Germans with the help of extra French troops who'd been sent out to the battlefield in taxi cabs! Florrie says they must have their own way of doing things over there, but it all sounded rather rum to me. I wondered why Mr Vye hadn't had to go to training camp first, like Isaac and Jim, but Hannah said it was because he'd been in an officer cadet force at school. Then we spent the rest of the time talking about the new autumn fashions, I must admit, and how we hoped the craze for tight hobble skirts was well and truly over.

By the time we'd arrived at the railway station, however, I was beginning to realise that the world had changed since I'd last been out and about in it. Edenvale's more of a big village than a town but, even so, there were recruiting posters up on all the lampposts, and a notice outside the village hall telling us it had been turned into a Red Cross Supply Depot. We saw two ladies wearing white armbands with a red cross who must have been volunteer nurses, and some men in khaki uniform were waiting to catch the London train.

'Look at that queue outside the grocer's shop!' my mother said. 'There doesn't seem to be much on the shelves - people must be stocking up. Maybe I should start getting a few things in.'

There was no escaping the war when our train

arrived at Hardingbridge, either. Coming out of the station, we heard the tramp-tramp of marching feet: a platoon of soldiers in uniform was heading towards us. We stopped to watch as they passed by, swinging their arms in time and stamping down their stout boots. They were singing 'It's a Long Way to Tipperary' (a song I'd never heard before, though I know it well enough now), their eyes fixed straight ahead as if they could see a battlefield at the end of the High Street and couldn't wait to reach it. People waved and cheered, and a little girl ran up with a bunch of flowers for the officer. You couldn't help but feel excited and proud that we had such fine, brave men ready to fight for our sake, and worried at the same time about what might happen to them. I took Tom's arm, wanting to hold on to him - although he could hardly have joined on the end of the line in a tweed jacket and flat cap, could he? His face gave nothing away; I had no idea what he was thinking.

And then something horrible happened. A young woman came walking towards Tom and me - quite a nice-looking girl, she was, in a bottle-green costume with a narrow skirt and a black hat trimmed with feathers. She had been smiling at first as though she knew us and was about to say hello, but as she approached, her expression changed to a look of such withering scorn, it shocked me to my bones.

'Don't you feel ashamed of yourself?' she

hissed at Tom, taking a white feather from her bag and thrusting it into his hand. 'This is to show the world what a coward you are.' She turned to me. 'You should find yourself a decent fellow who's not afraid to defend his country.' (I suppose she thought we were sweethearts.) And with that she stalked off, leaving us all too shocked to do anything other than stare after her.

'There's a nasty piece of work, if ever I saw one!' said my mother eventually. 'Don't pay her any attention, Tom.'

'Don't worry, I won't.' He laughed and tossed the feather aside; I saw it spiral down into the gutter.

I should have very much liked to run after that girl and box her ears. Who was she to call my brother a coward? She didn't know the first thing about him. That would only have made more of a scene, though, and Tom didn't seem to be half as angry and upset as the rest of us. I didn't know how he could shrug off the matter so lightly. Well, as it turned out, there was a reason for that - and we were shortly to find out what it was.

Chapter Four

As a whole, the country has answered splendidly to the call made on it ... but there is a type of able-bodied young man who seems content to look at others going without offering to go himself ... No task of the day is more important than that of rousing up these laggards. Most of them suffer from ignorance and lack of imagination.

From *Country Life,* 5 September 1914

'HURRY UP AND COME IN, you dozy lot! It's as cold as the Khyber Pass with that door wide open.'

Miss Eliza Everett was waiting for us in her backstage boudoir, where she would change before and after the show and where, Ma suspected darkly, she was in the habit of receiving visitors dressed in little more than a wrap - something no respectable lady would ever have contemplated. She was wearing her wrap now, a beautifully embroidered Chinese affair, but we were all family, so this was just about

44

acceptable. (Florrie and Alf had taken their seats in the music hall already. 'You'll want some time on your own,' they'd said, which conveniently gave them some time on their own, too.) Aunt Lizzie hugged me tight, swallowing me up in a cloud of rustling cream silk and the delicious scent of gardenias. Her dressing room's always warm, summer or winter, with silk shawls pinned to the walls and draped over lampshades which turn the light into a rosy glow. It was all so cosy and ladylike - except for Johnny Sylvester, her manager, waxing the ends of his moustache in front of the mirror. Ma can't bear him and I have my reservations, although he's always pleasant to us, in a smarmy sort of way.

'Now sit here and tell me your news, Pollyanna,' Aunt Lizzie said to Ma, patting the chair beside hers. 'Johnny, fetch some beer for the boys, there's a dear, and Hannah can help me dress my hair while Grace does something artistic with those flowers.' A chipped china jug on the table had been crammed full of red roses, drooping in the heat, with a card beside them which read 'From a true admirer'. There was nothing to trim the stems with so I had to snap the ends off as best I could, and wished I had my trusty vegetable knife with me.

We didn't really have much news, of course, apart from Ma going back to work and things being so difficult at the Hall with all the young men leaving. Now Da had even lost Bill from the stables: they'd introduced special bantam regiments for men who were too short for the regular army, so he'd upped and joined one of those. 'Goodness knows where we shall find anyone to replace him,' Da said, and I suddenly noticed how tired he was looking.

'What about you, young man?' Aunt Lizzie said to Tom. 'I should have thought you might have been off to fight by now. The army needs all the fine strong lads it can get.'

The room fell quiet. This was the question nobody had dared to ask; we all held our breath and waited for Tom's reply.

'Now you've spoilt my surprise,' he said, setting down his beer mug. 'I was going to break the news over supper. A crowd of us from the manor house have signed up with the Royal Field Artillery; Mr Ildersley had us driven to the recruiting office in his very own motor-car. We've been training near Ipswich for the last month.'

There was silence for a few seconds. 'Why didn't you say so before?' All the colour had drained from Ma's face. 'Leaving your job and not so much as a word to me or your father!'

'I wanted to tell you face to face.' He reached over and took her hand. 'Anyway, there hasn't been much time to write, what with all the drill, and marching, and rifle training. They keep us pretty busy but we manage to have a lark about, too. I'm with my pals, Ma - we look out for each other.'

She didn't say anything, just gazed at him as if the rest of the world had melted away and there was no one left but the two of them.

'Good for you!' Aunt Lizzie patted Tom on the back. 'William, you should be proud of your brave son.'

'And so I am,' Da said, shaking Tom's hand. 'When will you be off abroad, my boy?'

'I'm not sure. Not till after Christmas, at least,' he replied - whereupon Ma burst into tears.

'Now don't be like that, Pol.' Aunt Lizzie put an arm around her shoulder. 'You wouldn't think much of him if he didn't go, would you? There have to be men to fight. That's what this evening's about. Didn't you know? I'm the latest weapon in Lord Kitchener's recruiting campaign, would you believe. Just as well our Tom's signed up already, or you'd never speak to me again for taking him away.'

We didn't know quite what she meant at that point, but later on, after we'd taken our seats in the gallery, the crimson velvet curtains drew back to reveal Miss Eliza Everett on stage - with a couple of tables behind her and an army officer sitting at each one. She looked so beautiful, in a shimmering silver gown that fell to the floor and a couple of the red roses pinned in her dark hair, and when she started to sing, you could feel the tingles running up and down your spine. She opened the performance with a few old favourites like 'Show Me the Way to Go

Home' and 'Down at the Old Bull and Bush', which had everyone joining in, and then she began a new song, walking slowly down some steps leading from the stage into the audience. She looked along the front row at the men sitting there and sang especially to them, reaching out as if to draw them towards her. This is how the chorus went: 'Oh, we don't want to lose you, but we think you ought to go, For your King and your country, both need you so ...'

One man rose to his feet as though he'd been hypnotised, then another, and another, and Aunt Lizzie ushered them one by one towards the stage. She carried on down the aisle, still singing. More men got up as she approached: a couple here, another there, until soon there were too many volunteers to count. People clapped and patted them on the back as they made their way down the rows into the aisle, where the stream of men waiting to join up was fast turning into a queue, and Aunt Lizzie kept on walking and singing in that rich, thrilling voice of hers. She's like the Pied Piper, I thought to myself, only this time luring the grown-ups away. If I'd been a man, I would have answered the call too. Listening to Eliza Everett made you feel there was nothing you couldn't do. She was offering you the chance to leave behind your ordinary, everyday self and turn into some glorious hero whose name would live for ever. Who could turn that down?

Not Alf. I caught sight of his fair head, far

down below us (he and Florrie had been sitting in the stalls) as he pushed past everyone's knees and joined the line waiting to climb up on stage. His mother had kept him safe for as long as she could, but she was no match for my Aunt Lizzie.

None of us had much of an appetite at supper, except for Tom and Johnny Sylvester; anyway, we agreed the Chicken à la King wasn't a patch on Mrs Jeakes'. If it hadn't been for Aunt Lizzie telling us about her tour of America in the spring, we would have been a very quiet table in the middle of that noisy restaurant. I could count on the fingers of one hand the number of times we'd eaten out, yet I couldn't really enjoy it, knowing I'd have to say goodbye to my darling brother at the end of the evening. We didn't even know whether he'd be able to come home for Christmas.

'Now don't you go worrying about me,' he said, hugging me tight. 'I've got my chums with me - we'll be all right. Look after Ma, won't you?'

Aunt Lizzie had a different message with her farewell kiss. 'Everything's up in the air, Gracie,' she whispered in my ear, clasping me against the soft velvet bodice of her evening gown. 'You get out of that kitchen and make something of yourself.'

I was too anxious about Tom to consider my own prospects, however. It wasn't hard to see why he'd joined up, but I wished from the bottom of my heart that he didn't have to go. I was proud, half-excited, worried and frightened all at once - and Florrie must have felt the same about Alf. We had a little cry together before going to sleep that night. Then she blew her nose and told me we'd just have to get on with things and try to keep cheerful until our boys came back. Easier said than done, though. There wasn't a great deal to smile about in those dreary, grey weeks leading into winter. When Mr Fenton read out our tea-time reports from The Times, they seemed to be gloomier by the day. And then to add to Ma's worries, a letter came from Ivy with alarming news. She fished it out of her apron pocket and waved it indignantly at me, on my next afternoon off.

'Your daft sister's only gone and chucked her job in, too! "I have become a conductor on the number 19 omnibus for two pounds ten shillings a week." Have you ever heard of such a thing? Ivy, a bus conductor! The people she must come across.' My mother shuddered. 'You'd have to pay me a darn sight more than two pounds ten shillings to deal with the riff-raff in London. And she had such a good place in Kensington - she could have become a lady's maid, you know. Well, thank goodness you and Hannah have more sense, that's all I can say about the matter.' (Which unfortunately was not the case, because she kept going back over it for days to come.)

Working as a conductor on the number 19 omnibus sounded quite jolly to me. The kitchen was not such a pleasant place to be, what with Mrs Jeakes' temper, Florrie miserable from missing Alf, and the housekeeper, Mrs Maroney, turning up to check on us at every opportunity like the ghost of Christmas past. She'd started going through the tradesmen's bills, Florrie told me, and accusing Mrs Jeakes of throwing good food away. We even found her rooting around in the pigswill bucket one day.

Mrs Jeakes was outraged. 'What does she think I'm going to do with a load of old tea leaves? Sell them to the gipsies for fortune-telling?'

Dora brought us some news from the servants' hall about that. 'They're s-s-saying that His L-L-Lordship's t-trying t-t-to s-save m-m-money! That's w-w-why M-M-Mrs M-Maroney k-keeps going on about n-n-not w-w-w-wasting anything.'

There were still quite a few shooting parties that winter, however; Lord Vye's economies didn't stretch to cutting down on those. We were all rushed off our feet, from my father out in the stables to Mr Fenton up in the dining room. I was worried about Da. He was working so hard (they still hadn't been able to find a groom to replace Bill), and he'd been very quiet since we'd heard about Tom. I went to see him in the stables one afternoon, and found him washing mud off the gig in the yard.

'Shall I help you with that?'

'I'm sure you've got better things to do,' he replied, but I rolled up my sleeves and pitched in anyway. I had half an hour to spare; maybe if we spent some time together, he'd tell me what was on his mind. My father and I have always got along - we can usually manage to talk to each other about things that matter without having an argument, unlike me and Ma.

'So, what's the news from this neck of the woods?' I asked, after we'd been washing and wiping for a while.

'Haven't you heard? Monty's going back to France at the end of the week.'

Monty was Lord Vye's French chauffeur. His full name was Monsieur de Montrachet, which sounded so romantic, although unfortunately he wasn't the slightest bit handsome and it was hard to understand a word he spoke.

'Well, that was bound to happen,' I said. 'He must have been worried about his family. I'm surprised he's stayed as long as he has.'

'Thank you for that, Miss Know-It-All,' Father muttered. He threw his sponge down in the bucket, sending a wave of water slopping over the side. 'Maybe you can say what'll become of the rest of us, if you've brought your crystal ball along.'

Whatever could be the matter? He'd never spoken to me like that before, so narky and bitter. All I could do was stare at him, not knowing how to reply.

Da sat down on the mounting block with his head in his hands. 'Sorry, love,' he said after a moment, looking up. 'I'm that worried, I don't know which way to turn. Mr Braithwaite has told me they're advertising for a chauffeur and coachman all in one, to run the stables and drive the motor-car. When he comes, I shall have to work under him. And we'll probably have to let him take over our house.'

'Does Ma know about this?' I asked, stunned.

He shook his head. 'I haven't had the heart to tell her. Don't say anything, will you? Not for the time being, at least. She'll find out soon enough.'

We'd lived in the gate lodge for ten years, ever since my father had been made head coachman; I couldn't bear to think how Ma would feel about leaving it. There might be another cottage for us to rent on the estate, I suppose, although what we could afford was anybody's guess.

'Will you still be paid the same?' I asked.

He shook his head with a rueful smile. 'I'm not being paid the same now. Lord Vye's already cut my wages because I'm not a proper coachman any more.' He sighed. 'I've been thinking, maybe I should join the army. There's not much left for me here.'

'You couldn't volunteer!' I was horrified. 'You're too old, aren't you?'

'I'm not quite washed up yet. Can you imagine what it's like, having to stand aside for the young men to go past? Staying safe at home while my own son's facing heaven knows what? A lass gave me one of those white feathers the other day. She made me feel no higher than ninepence, I can tell you.'

'We're here, though, Da. Your family.' I made him shift up and sat beside him on the block. 'What would Ma do without you? She's already had to say goodbye to Tom - don't make her go through that again.'

Perhaps I should have encouraged him to sign up, but how could I, knowing how Ma would feel about it? My parents might have been married for twenty-three years but they're still forever sneaking kisses and worrying to death if the other's five minutes late. Ma would fall apart if Da went off to fight too. I had to keep him here with us.

'Listen,' I said, taking his arm so he'd look at me, 'Lord Vye doesn't need to advertise for a coachman-chauffeur. He's got the perfect person right here, under his nose.'

Da looked at me suspiciously. 'Who?'

'You, of course!'

He laughed. 'Whatever are you on about now? I can't drive a motor-car.'

'No, but you can learn. Get Monty to show you - it can't be that difficult. Why, you could even pay him.' The more I thought about the idea, the more sense it made. 'The Vyes are off to London this weekend, and they usually go up by train. If you buy the petrol and throw in a bit extra, I'm sure you could get Monty to stay on here till Sunday and take you out driving. At least that would be a start. Once His Lordship sees you know the basics, you can always practise.'

Father shook his head. 'I don't know, Grace. Could you really see me behind the wheel of one of those great things? You can't teach an old dog new tricks.'

'Of course you can!' I was beginning to lose patience. 'We're all doing different things - look at Ma and me in the gardens, and Tom learning how to be a soldier. The world's changing, Da, and we have to change with it or get left behind. Motoring's the way of the future, it has to be. Who'll bother with a horse and carriage when a motor-car is twice as fast and half as much bother? Apart from old Lady Vye, that is, and the world won't arrange itself according to her liking.'

Father pondered for a while until he managed to come up with another objection. 'We still don't have a groom, though. How could I manage the car and the horses, single-handed? I'm hardly keeping my head above water as it is.'

'You're bound to get some help sooner or later,' I said. 'It'll be a lot easier to find a groom than a chauffeur. Anyone who can drive has probably gone off to the Front by now.' The thing was, a most extraordinary idea had been growing in my head about that, too, but I wasn't ready to risk sharing it with my father. One step at a time…

'All right, I'll give it some thought,' he said eventually. 'I'm not saying yes, but I'm not saying no. You'll have to make do with that.'

Well, it was a start.

I should have liked to mull over this extraordinary idea of mine for a little while longer, but it was not to be. The very next day (a Thursday, it was - I remember clearly), Mrs Jeakes decided I was ready to make puff pastry, for eccles cakes. She'd gone through the recipe and I'd helped Florrie with it several times in the past, so I was quite confident. Sift the flour, mix it to a paste with water (not too much), chop a quarter of the butter into pieces, fold the paste over them and roll it out. Repeat four times until all the butter has been used up, remembering not to press too hard on the rolling pin and dusting it with flour each time.

All that buttering and flouring and rolling took for ever, but I was pleased with myself by the end, and presented the pastry slab to Mrs Jeakes with an idea that she might have to eat her words about my heavy hand.

'Right, now you can go and throw that straight into the pigswill,' she said, fixing me with her little curranty eyes. 'Start again from scratch, and do it properly this time.'

'What do you mean?' I stammered. 'What have I done wrong? I've been ever so careful with the rolling.'

'Oh, your rolling's all right, more or less. It's what happened before the rolling that I'm worried about. What did you do with the butter? Or rather, what did you forget to do with it?'

I'd cut the butter into quarters and then little pieces; what else should I have done? It had been covered in salt to keep fresh. Had I remembered to sluice off the salt? Surely I wouldn't have forgotten that! Mrs Jeakes was still glaring at me; I had to say something.

'I washed the butter and then cut it up - ' I began, hoping for the best.

She pounced. 'That's it, you daft nincompoop! How many times have I told you? You have to wring the butter out in a cloth to get rid of every drop of water and buttermilk, or the pastry ends up heavy as a housebrick. The only thing those eccles cakes would have been good for is firing at the Germans.'

I looked down at the pastry, which had taken me the best part of an hour to make. 'But you saw me, Mrs Jeakes,' I said, unable to hold back the words. 'You were watching all the time. Why didn't you stop me at the beginning?'

'Because this way, even a feather-brained halfwit such as yourself won't forget to wring out the butter in future!' she roared. 'Now get on with the next batch before I take that rolling pin to you.'

I started to untie my apron strings.

'What in heaven's name are you doing now?' Mrs Jeakes asked, her voice dangerously quiet.

I took the apron off and laid it on the table, and then I looked her straight in the face. 'It's time to give up the challenge, ma'am,' I said. (How did I find the nerve?) 'You've done your best with me, and I've done my best with you, but I'll never make a decent kitchenmaid and we both know it. You'd be better off without me.'

You could have heard a pin drop in that kitchen. Florrie stood at the other end of the table with her mouth open and a knife poised in mid-air above the chopping board. Dora froze in the scullery doorway. Mrs Jeakes stared at me for what seemed an age, but I didn't look away. Everything had become suddenly clear. I didn't give a fig for puff pastry, or duchesse potatoes, or stewed carrots, or any of it. Aunt Lizzie's words echoed in my head: it was time to get out of the kitchen and make something of myself.

'I don't doubt it,' Mrs Jeakes said at last. 'But may I enquire, as a matter of interest, what you intend to do with yourself instead?'

'I'm going to the stables, to work as a groom for my father,' I said.

The look on her face almost made my year and a half in the kitchen worthwhile. Almost, but not quite.

Chapter Five

The disappearance of the younger male servants in big establishments steadily continues. A post is waiting at the Labour Exchanges for a woman willing to go to the North of Ireland to do the work of a coachman and one, as has already been noted in The Times, has already replaced a man where a groom was kept at Taplow.

From *The Times*, 22 April 1915

'IT'S ABSOLUTELY OUT OF THE question.' Mr Braithwaite, the land agent at Swallowcliffe, stared at me with a very similar expression to the one that had been on Mrs Jeakes' face, when I stood in front of him an hour or so later in the estate office. 'What do you think Lord Vye would say about having a girl in his stables? You belong in the house.'

'But there are ladies working in the gardens

now, sir.' I tried not to sound too desperate. The thought of going back to Mrs Jeakes with my tail between my legs was not to be contemplated, and she probably wouldn't have let me over the threshold into the kitchen anyway. What could I do instead? Lie about my age and ask for a job on the omnibus alongside Ivy? Ma would be over the moon about that.

I had to win Mr Braithwaite round; he was already looking at the clock and pushing back his chair. Luckily he brushed a sheaf of letters off his cluttered desk in the process, which delayed him a little. I dropped to my knees and began picking them up. The office was in a dreadful mess, with papers heaped everywhere in drifts, and I'd been shocked by the state of the yard outside. Weeds were growing up through the cobblestones, the wood cart was half in and half out of the shed, and an untidy pile of logs sat waiting to be split by the carpenter's workshop, getting nicely soaked in the drizzle. Nobody seemed to be about. The woodsman and the carpenter must have gone the way of the garden lads: off on a troop ship to France.

'Please give me a chance, Mr Braithwaite,' I begged, shuffling the papers together and stacking them on top of an existing pile. 'I've been helping Father out in the stables since I was little. The horses know me, and I can ride perfectly well.'

'I don't doubt it,' he sighed, running his hands

through his oily black hair, 'and goodness knows, your father's in terrible need of a groom. But it's no job for a young lady, outside in all weathers and cleaning out dirty stalls - quite different from baking sponge cakes in a nice warm kitchen. You wouldn't last five minutes.'

I almost laughed. Is that how he imagined we passed our time? He should try skewering a whole suckling pig on a spit, or scouring a sinkful of copper pans with yeast and silver sand. 'Just give me a week to prove myself,' I said. 'That's all I'm asking.'

He got to his feet and started towards the door. 'I'm sorry, my dear. I honestly think you'd be better off back in the kitchen. Or why not see whether Mrs Maroney needs another housemaid?'

The thought of that made me desperate. I stood in front of the door, blocking his way. 'Please, just give me some kind of a test. I know! Let me clean up the yard. Then you'll see what I can do.'

He frowned at me. I widened my eyes and implored him with a smile, trying my best to look winsome. Mr Braithwaite has an eye for the ladies, it's well known. He danced with Florrie three times at the servants' party and tried to kiss her afterwards in the corridor, though he didn't take it to heart when she pushed him away. He's not so bad, all in all.

Then he smiled too, and my heart leapt. 'Well, I never could resist a pretty face,' he said, reaching past me to unhook his hat from the back of the door. 'I shall be away for a couple of hours. If you insist on pottering about here while I'm gone, I shan't stop you. But look, it's raining. Your hair will get wet, and you won't like that one little bit.'

'Oh, I'll manage,' I assured him. We went out of the office together and he locked the door behind me.

'Until later then, young lady,' he said, tipping his hat to me. 'If you're still here when I get back, that is.' I could hear him chuckling under his breath as he walked away.

I waited until he was quite out of the yard. Then I threw my shawl over my hair, rolled up my sleeves and set to work.

'Grace! Put that down, for goodness' sake, before you do yourself a mischief.'

The only one in danger of being hurt was Mr Braithwaite himself, grabbing my arm like that when I was about to bring down the axe. 'But I've nearly finished, sir,' I told him, slightly out of breath. 'Only a couple more logs to go. They'll need drying out for a while before they're ready for the fire, though.'

I'd found a couple of baskets in the carpenters' workshop, which were now brimming with freshly split logs. There had also been a hoe propped against the wall in the gardeners' bothy which I thought Mr McKinley wouldn't mind me borrowing (luckily I hadn't run into Ma), and all the weeds that had been standing up so proudly between the cobblestones lay in a forlorn pile on the compost heap. I'd swept the yard, carried a stack of broken chairs from the wood shed into the carpenters' workshop, and then rolled the cart into its proper position so the door could be properly bolted. That was a job and a half, but a combination of pulling and pushing with my whole weight against the heavy old thing had eventually got its wheels moving. The effort had half killed me, but I reckoned it was worth it for the sake of a job in the stables.

Mr Braithwaite stared around. The whole place looked quite different now that someone had paid it a little attention. 'Did you do all that yourself?'

I nodded.

'Who taught you how to use an axe?'

'My father. I'm a handy sort of person to have about the place, Mr Braithwaite, you'll see. I'm fit and strong, and a drop of rain doesn't bother me. I'm happy to muck out the stables, or clean harness, or wash down the carriages - whatever's required. And Father will keep me in line. We're used to working together.'

'I take it you've discussed this with him?'

I couldn't say yes but I couldn't bring myself to say no, either, so I made a kind of 'hmm-hmm' noise in my throat which could have meant anything, and hoped that would do.

Luckily, it seemed to. 'The final decision rests

with His Lordship, of course,' Mr Braithwaite said, still looking around the yard. 'I shall be seeing him later this afternoon and I'm prepared to put the idea to him. That's the best I can do. If you go to the stables for the time being, I'll let you know in due course.'

'Thank you, sir.' I curtseyed and hurried off before he could change his mind.

Da was nowhere to be seen in the stables and the gig wasn't in the coach-house; he must have been taking it out and about. I fetched a pitchfork and wheelbarrow and began mucking out the dirty stalls, exhausted though I was, wondering what I had started with one rash remark to Mrs Jeakes. The words had come out of my mouth before I'd thought twice, yet now the possibility of becoming a groom was within reach, my heart was set on it. This was what I wanted more than anything in my life before. There would be a few details to sort out, of course, like where I'd take my meals and what I should wear (my sodden, muddy dress flapped around my ankles and seemed to attract hay seeds like a magnet), but they weren't important. Working here with my father was all I cared about. Could such a wonderful thing ever happen?

Well, yes, apparently it could; I started the day as a kitchenmaid, and ended it as a groom.

'Whatever possessed you?' Florrie demanded, bursting into our bedroom that night to find me lying on the bed, resting my weary bones. 'Talking to Mrs Jeakes like that! She's been muttering about it ever since. She won't have you back, you know.'

'I don't want to come back,' I said, propping myself up on my elbows, and then I told Florrie and Dora the whole story.

'G-g-good f-f-f-or you,' Dora said, but Florrie wasn't nearly so enthusiastic.

'Look at the state you're in!' she said, picking up the hem of my dress between her finger and thumb. 'You'll have to give those hands a thorough scrub, and your frock's ruined. Why would you ever choose to work in such a dirty old place? It's not worth it, just to spite Mrs Jeakes.'

'That's not why I'm doing it!' I swung down my legs and sat up. 'Honestly, Florrie, it's my idea of heaven, spending all day in the stables. It might not suit you, but everyone's different, aren't they? And you have to admit, I was never a very good kitchenmaid.'

'That's true enough.' She sat on her bed and looked at me. 'It still doesn't seem right, though, having a girl for a groom. What did your father say?'

'Oh, Father's so grateful for any help that he came round to the idea in the end. Besides, he probably thinks he can keep a closer eye on me if we're working together. It's all turning out perfectly, Florrie - I can't tell you how happy I am! I'm to be given two pairs of riding breeches and some decent leather boots, and Da's going to fetch our dinner from the yardhouse so we can eat in the harness-room.' (The yardhouse was where the remaining outdoor staff - the gamekeeper, gardener, handyman and so on - took their meals, but they were all men and it wouldn't have been right for me to join them.)

'Riding breeches!' Florrie was scandalised. 'You can't go about in those! Whatever will people say?'

'Breeches will be much handier around the stables than a print frock, and Her Ladyship thinks so too. I've never got on with riding side-saddle.'

'Well, I'm glad you're all cock-a-hoop, though heaven only knows why,' Florrie said, taking up her towel. 'I should imagine you won't give us poor creatures a second thought, slaving away in the kitchen, but we shall miss you. Won't we, Dora?'

Dora nodded vigorously.

How could I have been so stupid? Crowing about my new job without a care for anyone else's feelings. 'But you'll still be seeing more than enough of me,' I told them both, 'since I'm to carry on sleeping here. Will you visit the stables sometimes, too, for a proper chat?'

Florrie sniffed. 'Perhaps, if we're not too busy.'

I fetched my towel too and linked arms with her so we could go to the bathroom together. 'I shall miss you like anything,' I said when Dora was out of earshot, not wanting her to feel left out. 'Of course I will. Think of all the laughs we've had together behind old Jeaksy's back. I won't be far away, though.'

'I know,' she said, sitting on the edge of the bath while I started to wash in the basin. (The colour of that water!) 'It's just, what with Alf going off, and now you … It won't be the same in the kitchen if you're not there. Everything's up in the air, Grace, and I don't like it.'

'It'll all work out for the best, you'll see,' I promised, drying my hands and coming to give her a hug. 'Just because things are different, doesn't mean they'll be worse.'

'Do you really think so?' She held me tight. 'Sometimes it feels as though I'm at the edge of a cliff and there's nothing I can do to stop myself falling over - only wait for it to happen.'

My heart went out to Florrie, but my head was too full of plans and possibilities to feel so hopeless. It seemed to me that I was leaping forward, like a salmon swimming upstream, and how could that not be exciting? Doing something - anything, almost - was better than sitting around, moping. Of course I was worried to death about Tom and this dreadful war, but surely it was better to seize whatever opportunities came my way than to let them pass by. Besides, what was the point in us both being sad? So I did my best to cheer Florrie up. When we were back in the bedroom, I made her repeat everything that Mrs Jeakes had said after I'd left the kitchen. There's no one who can imitate Mrs Jeakes like she does, and I think she went to sleep in a happier frame of mind.

Florrie wasn't the only one to be less than delighted at the prospect of my new position. Ma had to be sat down with a strong cup of tea in the harness-room to get over the shock of seeing me in my breeches, forking up dirty straw into the wheelbarrow. She'd dropped by the stables unexpectedly to bring Da the snap tin of bread and cheese for elevenses he'd left at home that morning.

'How could you let her do it, Will?' she asked him, hardly able to bring herself to look at me. 'You should have sent her back to the kitchen, lickety split. The idea of it! Our little Grace, dressed up like a man and getting her hands filthy dirty. She should be turning into a young lady, not a labourer.'

'No one'll see me in breeches except Father,' I said, trying to reassure her. 'I'm to be given a riding habit for driving the gig. Anyway, you're working in the gardens. How is this any different?'

'Because I'm a married woman, and I'm only doing my bit to help the country in an emergency. You had a good place in the kitchen, my girl, and you've thrown it away. What's going to happen when our boys come back? Have you thought about that? You'll be out on your ear in no time, and let me tell you this - ' she leaned forward and wagged a warning finger under my nose, 'no one's going to want a wife who doesn't know how to cook and smells of horses.'

'Now, Polly, that's a long way off,' Da broke in. 'Grace is old enough to make up her own mind, and if she wants to work in the stables then I'm not going to stand in her way. I'm too glad of the help, to be honest. She'll make a first-rate groom and that's what matters to me. Surely it's better she should be happy here than miserable in the kitchen?'

A first-rate groom! It was so wonderful to think I might actually be good at something that I couldn't help beaming. And indeed, my new place turned out to be everything I could have hoped for. To begin with, anyway. We had four horses to look after - Bella (Lady Vye's hunter), Moonlight, old Daffodil and Cracker, who had recently been bought for the Vyes' older son - and two ponies - Cobweb and little Pippin, who pulled the mowing-machine - which was just about manageable between the two of us. First thing, Da would open up the stables and help me sweep them out, then we'd take Bella and Moonlight or Cracker for a ride if they needed the exercise, which was hardly like work at all. After that it was time for feeding and grooming the horses, turning those out to grass who weren't wanted that day, and then mucking out the stalls, soaping and polishing in the harness-room.

We ate our meals together very companionably there, for it's such a cosy place. There's a fireplace and a boiler for preparing hot mashes and warming the hot-water pipes, a comfortable armchair beside it, and a stag's head with spiky antlers mounted on the wall above - keeping a kindly eye on us all, or so it seems to me. I did miss having a friend like Florrie to talk to, but it was such a relief not to have Mrs Jeakes watching my back, despairing over everything I did. If Da had any advice, he'd tell me straight out and I'd usually remember next time; it was as simple as that.

'I shall be leaving you in charge of the stables shortly,' he said to me on the Saturday, after we'd given the horses their hay and oats. 'I have to go out for a while.'

I'd been careful not to nag him about learning to drive; once you've put an idea in my father's head, he needs time to think it over. I couldn't resist raising my eyebrows at him, though.

'You win. Monty's going to take me for a spin in the motor-car,' he said, laughing at my expression. 'And if I manage to stay on the road, we shall be out for the whole of tomorrow, too.'

'There you are! You'll be driving by yourself in no time,' I said, thoroughly delighted.

Having the stables to myself was quite a treat. In the afternoon, being well ahead with my chores, I took Cracker out for a ride. She was a lively character, although I was beginning to get the measure of her. Both the Vye sons would soon be home from school for the Christmas holidays, which was just as well;

they could help exercise the horses. The weather had turned bright and frosty, and I couldn't believe Lord Vye was actually paying me to ride through his beautiful grounds. Then who should I find on my return to the stables but Philip Hathaway, feeding Moonlight a carrot. The sight of him brought back such a flood of uncomfortable memories that I felt myself blushing as I jumped off Cracker and led her into the stable block.

'Hello, Grace,' Philip said. 'So you managed to escape from the kitchen for good? Well done! You look very fetching in those breeches.'

'Lord Vye's given me permission to wear them,' I said, my cheeks hotter than ever. Luckily, unbuckling the girth and heaving off Cracker's saddle gave me an excuse to hide my face. 'They're more practical than a skirt.'

'I think it's an excellent idea.' He smiled at me. 'Here, let me give you a hand with that.' And he made as if to take the saddle out of my arms.

'It's all right, thank you, sir. I can manage.'

'Still as prickly as ever, I see.' He followed me towards the harness-room. 'Why don't we declare a truce? You should be pleased with me. It took some persuading, but I think my uncle finally believes it was you who rescued his horse, and now he knows why. Didn't you wonder what was happening?' He opened the door for me and we went through together.

'Thank you,' I said, 'but I'm trying to forget about that and I'd be grateful if you would too.'

He laughed. 'That's a pity, I should say it was your finest hour. And now here you are in the stables, doing the unexpected thing all over again. I take my hat off to you, Grace - you're full of surprises. '

I stowed Cracker's saddle on its wooden tree and put her bridle to one side for cleaning later. 'And what can I do for you, sir? Did you want to go for a ride?'

'I thought I might take Moonlight out, if that's all right, although I insist on carrying his saddle. Which one is it?'

I was too quick for him, though, and had the saddle down in a second. 'You must let me do my job, sir. It's what I'm here for.'

'I suppose so,' he said, jumping up. 'But in return, you have to promise to stop calling me "sir" all the time, as I seem to remember mentioning before.'

'What shall I call you, then?' I asked, looking for Moonlight's bridle.

'How about Philip? At least when there's nobody around. I hate all this "sir" business - we've known each other too long for that.'

That's one thing I'll say for the Hathaways: they treat everyone just the same. 'I'll take my coffee in the library, Fenton,' that's His Lordship's idea of conversation with one of us. But Philip's mother always stops by to see Ma when she's visiting the Hall, and they chat away in the kitchen over a cup of tea like nobody's business. They made friends when they were young, and Mrs Hathaway's evidently the sort of person who doesn't pretend to forget about that. She trained as a doctor, which is out of the ordinary to begin with, and she does some sort of work at the cottage hospital, so she's seen a little of the world that most of us live in.

Philip held the door for me again, and talked all the way back to the stable block and for most of the time it took to saddle up Moonlight. He'd just finished the first term of a medical degree at Oxford University, apparently, and was planning to become a doctor like his father.

'What about the war?' I couldn't help asking. 'Won't you be going off to fight?'

'I haven't decided yet,' he said, which surprised me a little. Whatever my reservations about him, I'd have thought he'd was the type to do his duty.

'Why not?'

'I'm not quite sure I agree with this war.'

That wasn't much of an answer. 'I shouldn't think there's many who do,' I said, walking around Moonlight's head to look him in the face. 'But it's started now and we all have to do our bit. Do you think the Huns are going to march through Belgium and France and then stop at the Channel? What will you say when they're knocking on our front door?

"Do come in and make yourselves at home?"'

Why, German warships had even started shelling Hartlepool and a couple of other towns along our east coast. One hundred and thirty-seven people had lost their lives: not soldiers or sailors but ordinary people like us, going about their daily business. A girl had been killed scrubbing her front step. The war wasn't in some faraway country any more, but right here, at home!

'And who are these dreadful Huns, bayoneting babies and old women and carrying out all these terrible atrocities we read about in the newspaper?' he asked. 'Do you really think their soldiers can be so very different from ours?'

'Of course they are! They're Huns, aren't they? You just said it yourself. And they're the ones who've started all this off.'

'They're only doing what they're told, the same as our troops.' He untwisted the cheek strap on Moonlight's bridle. 'Perhaps we should let the generals fight it out with each other. They might not be so quick to declare war if no one was prepared to back them up.'

I had no idea what he was talking about. 'We have to back them up! What else are we going to do? Pretend it isn't happening?'

The thought of Tom, and Alf, and all the thousands of other brave young men preparing to defend their country, even sailing over from abroad (not to mention veterans like Colonel Vye) while Philip Hathaway stuck his head in the sand at Oxford University and got on with life as usual - well, it made me want to spit. I thought he was just making up excuses not to fight. A rotten coward, in other words. And if he went around saying that kind of thing in public, he'd most probably be lynched.

'Here you are,' I said, handing him the reins. 'Have a nice ride. Sir.'

He led Moonlight over to the mounting block without another word. I pulled on the opposite stirrup while he got into the saddle and then tightened the girth.

'Can we not try to be friends, Grace?' he asked, looking down at me when he was done. 'We shall be seeing a lot more of each other soon, and I'd like it if we could get on.'

But I merely turned on my heel and walked away, too angry to wonder what he might have meant. We hardly spoke when he came back from his ride, and I was still out of sorts when Da returned from the driving lesson. At least that didn't seem to have gone too badly.

'I got the thing started,' he reported, 'and drove a couple of miles. The darn clutch pedal's tricky to manage - I shall need some more practice before I can get the hang of it properly. There are so many things to think about at the same time, that's the trouble, what with the clutch, and the gear lever, and steering. It's quite a performance.'

I could see he was enthusiastic, though; he told me that Monty had agreed to take him out the whole of the next day because he 'showed promise' (at least, Da thought that's what he said). Since it was Sunday and I had the afternoon off, they said I could sit in the back for a little while, so long as I didn't speak or otherwise be a distraction. My first trip in a motor-car! It was wonderful in every way. The smell of the leather seats, the purr of the engine as we sailed down the drive with the wind in our faces, and then the sight of the open road stretching out for miles ahead, beckoning us on ... I shan't forget it, as long as I live.

'You were right, Grace,' my father said to me that night. 'People will never stop riding horses, but there's something to be said for the motor-car. I'm going to talk to Mr Braithwaite about the chauffeur's job. I shall need a few more lessons, but I may be able to manage it.'

He was to be disappointed, however. Mr Braithwaite came to talk to Da, rather than the other way round. He said that a chauffeur had just been appointed with overall responsibility for the stables, and that he was dreadfully sorry, but we would have to move out of the gate lodge directly after Christmas.

Chapter Six

I have not washed for a week, or had my boots off for a fortnight ... It is all the best fun. I have never felt so well, or so happy, or enjoyed anything so much. It just suits my stolid health, and stolid nerves, and barbaric disposition. The fighting-excitement vitalises everything, every sight and word and action.

From a letter by Captain Julian Grenfell to his parents from Flanders, 3 November 1914. He died of his wounds in May 1915, aged 27.

THE NEW CHAUFFEUR WAS CALLED Jim Gallagher. He was good-looking, and didn't he know it: curly brown hair and eyes so blue you couldn't help but notice them. If he smiled (which didn't often happen), it was as if he'd decided you were worthy of some wonderful present. And he only smiled with his mouth. Those pale eyes stayed cold, looking past your shoulder to see if anyone more important was about. In fact, the only thing to be said in his favour was that he had consented to sleep in a room over the stables until his wife and family arrived after Christmas, when they would take possession of the gate lodge. I disliked him on sight, and nothing he did over the next few weeks made me change my mind. You could tell straight away he didn't care about horses, for one thing.

'I shall inspect the stables every morning,' he told us straight off. 'If there are any decisions to be made, we can talk about them then. Apart from that, I'll be spending most of my time on the motor-car - it's not been left in good condition and needs a lot of work. I shan't want to be bothered, so don't come running to me with every little problem. Understand?'

'How can you let him talk to you like that?' I asked Da when we were on our own. 'Doesn't he realise you've been running the stables for ten years? You've forgotten more about this place than he'll ever know.'

He shrugged. 'The man's been put over me, so I shall just have to get used to it. Still, at least it sounds like he'll leave us alone.'

That was true. We were able to get on with our work in peace for the most part, and carry on taking our meals together as usual - although Mr Gallagher (who ate with the others in the yardhouse) seemed somehow to sense the moment we sat down and would come marching in with some order that he should have given us hours earlier. The harness-room wasn't our cosy sanctuary any longer, not when he could suddenly turn up there without warning.

One day he met Florrie on her way out as he was coming in; she had the afternoon off and the three of us had shared a quick bite of dinner together. He looked at the remains of our meal on the table and then at me. 'You'd better not be wasting all day gossiping, young lady, or I shall have you back with your friends in the kitchen on a permanent basis. It still doesn't seem right to me that a slip of a girl should be doing man's work. There must be a strong lad somewhere who'd be glad of the job.'

'Not that we could find in two months of looking,' Da said. 'Anyway, Grace is as good a groom as anyone could want. If she starts slacking off, she'll have me to reckon with, don't you worry.'

I had found it hard to cope for the first few days, what with all that heavy labour and hours spent riding after being so long out of practice. Now, though, there were muscles in my arms and colour in my cheeks from being out in the fresh air, and I managed my chores without too much trouble. I put in an honest day's work for my pay, as Mr Gallagher would know if he did his job properly and paid any sort of attention to the stables. He'd taken against me by now, though, and I knew why. One morning he had come to inspect the place when Da was out with the gig (as quite often happened), so it was my turn to show him round and take his instructions - once we had got one thing settled.

'Would you mind putting out your cigarette, please, Mr Gallagher?' I asked, smelling tobacco smoke on the air before he'd even walked in.

'I won't be staying long,' he said, puffing away as he strode towards the stalls. 'The muck heap's too full. Take a barrow load round to the kitchen garden for compost, will you?'

'I'm sorry, sir,' I said, standing in his way. 'Nobody smokes in here, that's the rule.'

It was hard to believe he could do such a stupid thing, even out of forgetfulness. There was too great a risk of fire, with all that straw about and a full hayloft up above to feed the flames. I knew my father would say as much to anyone, no matter who they were.

Mr Gallagher stared at me. Then he took another pull on the cigarette and sent three perfect smoke rings sailing into the air, one after another. 'So now you're giving out orders, are you?' he said, when he'd quite finished. 'Strange, I thought that was my job.'

I couldn't believe he was being so awkward! It made me even more determined not to back down. 'Lord Vye insists, I'm afraid.' (Well, he might, at a pinch.) 'I'll lose my job if he hears there was anyone smoking in here.'

'And we can't have that, can we? Not when you're such a very good worker. According to your father, that is, and why would he lie?' He put his face next to mine; I could smell the rank smoke on his breath and see a shred of tobacco on his tongue. 'I'm keeping a close eye on you, young lady, and don't you forget it for one second. Now get that muck heap in order, double quick.' He tossed the cigarette into a bucket of clean water and strode out of the stables, leaving me to lean against the wall before my knees gave way. My heart was beating like the clappers; Mr Gallagher wasn't the type to be shown up by a girl and get over it in a hurry.

'It's so unfair,' I complained to my father, after I'd told him the whole story. 'Why should we have to take orders from a jumped-up ignoramus like him? Think of all the years you've been working for Lord Vye!'

'We both know His Lordship doesn't care about the stables. He's only interested in that motor-car, and he wants a nice-looking chap to drive him about in it.'

Da put a hand to touch the scar that puckered up one cheek, probably not even aware of what he was doing. Years ago, he'd broken up a drunken fight and been cut about the face, which was why he'd had to stop working in the house (footmen having to look presentable). Becoming a groom and then coachman was much more to his taste, though, since he'd always loved horses and learned to ride as a young boy, growing up next door to a farm.

'I'm sure your mother and I won't end up out on the street,' he went on. 'We can probably bunk down over the stables until another place comes up.'

'You don't think Lord Vye's paying you back for what happened in the summer with the Colonel's horse, do you?' I asked. This uncomfortable idea had been in my mind for a while. 'There'll be consequences,' Da had said at the time, and now here he was, having to give up his home. Was it because of what I had done?

'I can't see His Lordship harbouring a grudge about that. Mr Gallagher needs a cottage - he has a wife and two little ones coming to join him in the new year, so it makes sense for them to have the gate lodge. We're rattling around in it now, with you children grown up and gone.'

'And when are you going to tell Ma she's to pack her bags and move out? You can't keep putting it off for ever.'

He sighed. 'I know. Let's all have a happy Christmas first, though, eh? I don't want anything to spoil that. If your mother thinks Mr Gallagher's going to carry on living over the stables, that's fine by me. She doesn't need to know any different for the moment.'

Grace's Story

I think it was at the back of everyone's mind that this might be the last Christmas we would spend together as a family, with Tom going to the Front soon afterwards. Ivy had a week off from the number 19 omnibus so she'd be coming down from London, and Hannah had been given the Christmas Day afternoon as a holiday. She was very busy because Mrs Vye had just had her baby: another little girl. 'Mr Vye's hoping for a few days' leave to come and see her,' Hannah told us when she came by the gate lodge on a Sunday afternoon. 'She's a darling, Ma - nearly seven pounds! And a fine pair of lungs.'

'Well, it's nice to hear some good news for a change,' my mother said. 'We should try and forget our worries for a while and think how much there is to be thankful for. Ivy will be home soon, and Tom staying for two whole days - it's going to be a lovely Christmas, I can feel it in my bones.'

But another worry had come along to bother me, quite apart from Mr Gallagher, and this one was no easier to forget. You see, I was in much closer contact with the family now than had ever been the case in my previous life as a kitchenmaid. Lady Vye would often take Bella out in the afternoon and I would ride alongside her to open the gates and be on hand in case of accidents. It was hard to keep up on Moonlight or Cracker when she went off for a gallop, but we usually managed to meet up again sooner or later. Lord Vye's two sons were home from boarding school for the Christmas holidays, and they were often in the stables as well. I could tell that the older one, Charles, had the same feelings about a girl working there as Mr Gallagher. He was fifteen, the same age as me, and quite the young lord already; his mother had to speak sharply to him over the way he ordered my father about.

'Mr Stanbury to you, Charles,' she said. 'And if you want Cracker saddled up, please ask Grace to oblige. That's her job.'

Of course he hated being shamed in front of me and became even ruder when his mother wasn't there. Whenever he came back into the yard after a ride, I was expected to drop everything and run to take the horse; he never stayed to give her a pat and a kind word. His younger brother Lionel was a much more likeable, gentle boy - he seemed to have more of his mother in him. Then again, perhaps being the younger son is an easier part to play. Charles would inherit Swallowcliffe one day; he probably thought he had to make his mark with us servants and wasn't sure how to do it. My mother had once told me that she thought Lady Vye had been trying to have a baby for years, and they must have been getting desperate by the time Charles came along. Perhaps it was natural that he should have been spoiled a little.

The way Master Charles treated me did not matter so much, however; it was the way he treated Cracker that I found hard to take. Horses are the same as people: they have their own individual characters, their particular likes and dislikes. Cracker's a fidgety young madam, in need of a sensible rider with a steady hand before she can settle into her stride. Charles wouldn't give her a moment to catch her breath, though - as soon as he was up in the saddle, he'd be yanking the reins about and kicking her on. I could see from her eyes how much she hated it, and she didn't take kindly to the whip, either. It didn't make her go any faster, it just made her hate Master Charles. They were a mismatched pair if ever I saw one, and it was a shame, because he'd ruin Cracker's soft mouth and spoil her temper for good if he carried on like that.

I was surprised that Lady Vye didn't take her son in hand, but they didn't often go out riding together and Charles probably kept his temper in check when they did. So all I could do was try to calm Cracker down when he brought her back. I'd sponge her heaving, sweaty sides with warm water and cover her up with a thick blanket, stuffing a layer of straw underneath if it was particularly cold, then give her some fresh water to drink (warmed up with a drop from the kettle), and a bran mash to soothe her mouth. Poor thing, I did feel sorry for her.

A few days before Christmas, the whole household was summoned to the chapel for another talk from Lord Vye. We had been expecting some sort of announcement about our servants' dinner, which surely wouldn't be held this year, not with the war going on. Christmas was usually a grand time for us at Swallowcliffe. On the morning of Christmas Eve there would be a party for the tenants' children, with Lady Vye giving out presents and organising wonderful rowdy games. Then the carol singers would come, followed by a huge dinner at mid-day in the ballroom for all the servants and tenants. There was always as much roast venison, beef and pork as you could eat, and every kind of vegetable under the sun. We didn't have to lift so much as a finger - not even down in the kitchen. All the food was ordered in from London, along with a French chef to prepare it, twenty footmen to wait on us hand and foot, and a team of maids to clear up afterwards.

It wouldn't seem right to have such a great celebration with so many empty seats around the table, and so many men spending their Christmas sitting in a trench with nothing but bully beef and hard biscuits for dinner. No one was surprised when Lord Vye told us the children's party was to be the only one held this year, with the games quieter than usual as a mark of respect. We thought that was that, but then he went on to take us all by surprise. I would never have guessed what he was about to say next, not in a hundred years.

'I have some important news that will affect each and every one of us. As you know, this great house has been home to many generations of the

Vye family, and also to their servants. The time has now come, however, to open our door to others. I have to tell you that Swallowcliffe Hall is to become a convalescent home for wounded officers, for the duration of this war. It will be a haven where they can recover from their injuries in peace and tranquillity before returning to the heat of battle - or being discharged from the army, as the case may be.'

A gasp of surprise had run around the hall; I caught Florrie's eye and we stared at each other, flabbergasted. Lord Vye held up a hand for quiet. 'There is no need for alarm. I should like everyone to carry on working here as usual, although some of you may find that your duties will change. My sister, Mrs Hathaway, will supervise the medical arrangements and we shall have a team of volunteer nurses to look after the men. The family will continue living here, and the Dowager Lady Vye will also be returning to the Hall, since the Dower House is to be used for nurses' accommodation. My wife and I will not be adding to your burden of care, however. We shall be leaving for an extended tour of the United States in the new year.'

Well! How about that? We filed out behind Mr Fenton and went back to our duties not knowing quite what to think. Of course it was only right that Swallowcliffe should be put to good use; we had heard that the government was taking over property like motor-cars and buses if there was a need for them in the war (Lord Vye had been lucky to keep his Rolls-Royce), and even some buildings where soldiers could train and be billeted. Requisitioning, that's what it was called. All the same, this was going to have a great effect on us. There might be nurses to look after the men, but who was going to cook and clean for them? How could we cope with all the extra work? It also seemed strange that the Vyes should have picked this moment to leave the country - not to mention dangerous. I couldn't wait for Florrie to come and bring me some gossip from the servants' hall.

She picked her way through the puddles in the yard that afternoon with a full report. 'They say His Lordship's the one behind this trip to America. Lady Vye's worried about going away at a time like this, but her father's ill and Lord Vye thinks they should visit him before it's too late.' She lowered her voice, even though there was no one but the two of us in the stables; Father would be busy for hours, bringing some of old Lady Vye's things up to the Hall in the dog-cart. 'Dora said Bess heard Mr Fenton tell Mrs Maroney that Lord Vye wanted to make sure Mr Brookfield - that's Her Ladyship's father - wasn't going to die and leave his fortune to the church. They say he's got very religious in his old age. Mr Fenton thinks that if some money doesn't come to the Hall pretty soon, we shall all be in trouble. Lord Vye only went and invested in some German business last year, and now he stands to lose the lot.'

'But don't you think it's too risky to sail anywhere with those U-boats about in the Channel?' I asked, leaning on the broom.

'The Vyes'll be leaving from Liverpool,' Florrie replied. 'That's the other side of the country from where the bombing is, and maybe things aren't so bad there. Even so, I wouldn't fancy it myself. Oh, look, here come the boys - better make myself scarce. Toodlepip, Gracie.' She went off humming, in high spirits because Alf would soon be home on leave from training camp.

Picking out Cracker's hooves that morning, I'd noticed that one of her shoes was coming loose. I'd hammered the clench back down, though there was no knowing how long it would hold, and mentioned to Mr Gallagher that we should ask the farrier to call. He wouldn't hear of it.

'The man was here only last week, and His Lordship's told me to cut down on the stable bills. This place is costing a fortune to run! I'm not having him round for one loose shoe - you'll have to wait until he comes again.'

I tried to mention the matter to Charles when I handed Cracker over, but he didn't pay me any attention and had taken her off before I could even finish the sentence. Still, with a bit of luck the shoe would stay on for a bit longer; if she dropped it, he'd just have to bring her back. With this in mind,

I wasn't entirely surprised to hear him shouting for me from the yard, an hour or so later. Hurrying out of the harness room, I found him leading Cracker along on foot. She was hobbling along like some broken old nag.

'Damn horse cast a shoe,' he said. 'Why did you saddle her up if she wasn't fit to ride?'

'I did try to tell you it was loose this morning.' I took the reins from him, worried by the foam at Cracker's mouth and her rolling eyes. They'd obviously had quite some battle. 'Shh, old girl, steady now. Let's get you inside and take a look.'

'She's vicious and lazy, that's what the matter,' Charles said. 'And you're not taking proper care of her, which doesn't help. Jim would never have let me go out on a horse in that state.' And off he went, back to the house.

'Don't worry, I'll put Cobweb away,' Lionel offered. I could have kissed him.

'What happened, Master Lionel? Why is Cracker in such a state?'

He hesitated for a moment. 'I don't think we noticed straight away that her shoe had come off. Charles thought she was just being naughty when she wouldn't go.'

It took a long time and a great deal of patient coaxing before Cracker would let me anywhere near that particular leg. When at last I managed to lift it up, I could see why she was in such distress. Her hoof had been split down to the quick, and the soft part of her foot badly cut underneath. She must have been ridden hard over rough, stony ground to do such damage. No wonder she wouldn't cooperate; the pain must have been awful.

I could have kicked myself for having let this come about. Maybe I shouldn't have let Cracker out until the farrier had seen her, like Charles had said. But I really didn't think she'd cast the shoe so soon - and even if she had, he should have felt it immediately. I felt as though I had failed the poor horse. Well, I'd make sure that never happened again.

Chapter Seven

Now, dearest Mum, keep your heart up, and trust in Providence: I am sure I shall come through all right. It is a great and glorious thing to be going to fight for England in her hour of desperate need and, remember, I am going to fight for you, to keep you safe.

From a letter written by Second Lieutenant Cyril Rawlins, December 1914

I FOUND MR GALLAGHER sitting in the small shed next to the barn where the Rolls Royce was kept, which he had cleared for his own use. He'd fitted it out with a table and chair, and a wood-burning stove to keep the place warm. His feet were up on the table and he was reading a newspaper, swigging from a small silver hip flask.

'I thought I told you not to come interrupting me, Missy,' he said, glowering.

'I'm sorry, sir, but Cracker's cast that shoe and cut her foot. I've tied it up in a poultice but Mr Johnson needs to take a look.'

'Didn't you hear what I said this morning? We're not having the farrier round again until after Christmas, and that's final. Give her a few days' rest, and then he can look at her with the others next time - it won't kill the horse to wait a few days.'

How could he say that without even having seen her? I was sure that we needed Mr Johnson to look at Cracker now, not in a week's time. He was as much of a horse doctor as a farrier, and Father relied on his advice. I tried again. 'Mr Gallagher, Cracker's been hurt, she needs more than rest. I think - '

'I don't care what you think.' He belched. 'Didn't you listen? The decision's been made.' He took a fob watch out of his waistcoat pocket. 'Lord and Lady Vye are coming to my office in a minute to talk about a new motor-car for Her Ladyship, and I don't want them to see you hanging about. Get on with your work.' He took a peppermint out of his coat pocket and popped it in his mouth. 'What are you waiting for? Off you go.'

So off I went, knowing I'd get no change out of him. It wasn't the end of the matter, though; I'd made Cracker a promise and I wasn't going to let her down. When the Vyes came walking past the stables a little while later on their way to Mr Gallagher's 'office', I was sweeping the yard, ready to waylay them.

'Hello, Grace,' Lady Vye smiled, and then asked (as I knew she would), 'How are you?'

'I'm a little worried about Cracker, M'lady,' I said quickly, in a low voice. 'I wonder if you'd be so good as to come and see her?'

Her face changed instantly. 'Of course. Edward, I'll be five minutes. You can start talking to Mr Gallagher without me.'

Lord Vye looked rather put out, but we hurried into the stables together before he could say anything. 'These men and their motor-cars,' Lady Vye confided. 'I'd far sooner come and see the horses, to tell you the truth.'

Cracker was lying down on the straw in her stall. She put her ears back when we came in, but eventually she let us examine the injured foot. Lady Vye was very gentle and took no longer than was necessary. 'This is dreadful,' she said, turning to me. 'How did such a thing happen, Grace? Were you riding her at the time?'

'Master Charles had taken her out, and we think it took him a while to notice the shoe had come off.' I've never liked blowing the whistle on anybody, but the truth had to be told. 'Perhaps Master Lionel can tell you more about it. But I think Mr Johnson really ought to see her, ma'am, if you'd agree.'

'Well of course he should, there's no need to ask me for permission. Hasn't your father gone to fetch him already? Oh no, he's busy this afternoon, I forgot.' She got up, dusting down her frock. 'I know! Mr Gallagher will be driving us to the Cunninghams for dinner shortly. You can ride in the front of the motor with him and he'll drop you off at the farrier's - it's on our way.'

I could hardly object, although my stomach turned over at the very thought. Mr Gallagher was bound to find out sooner or later what I'd done, but Lady Vye ordering him to drive me to Mr Johnson's door was rubbing salt into the wound. If looks could kill, I'd have dropped down stone dead from the way he glared at me when I climbed up into the motor-car an hour later. I kept as far away from him as possible, sitting on my hands so he wouldn't see them shaking and wishing I could disappear in a puff of smoke. To my dismay, he got out of the motor with me when we arrived at the farrier's, 'to make sure I explained things properly'. It was dark by now. He took my arm, gripping it so tightly I had the marks of his fingers for days afterwards, and drew me to one side once we were well out of earshot.

'Now listen to me carefully, because I'm only going to say this once. You might think you've been pretty clever, running to Lady Vye, but I've got His Lordship's ear and he pays your wages. I'd already decided one of you had to go, you or that pug ugly father of yours. Well, now you've settled the question for me. You're not up to the job, and that's what I shall tell anyone who asks. By the time I come back tonight, there's to be no sign of you or your belongings anywhere in those stables. I want to pretend you never existed. If I ever set eyes on you again, you'll wish you hadn't been born.'

'Grace! I wasn't expecting you till tomorrow,' my mother said when I appeared in her kitchen that night. 'Got some extra time off, have you? That's nice. Ivy's upstairs, getting ready for bed. She's got a terrible cold. Well, of course she would have, being exposed to all those - '

'All those what?' My sister's voice floated through the door, followed by Ivy herself, in a nightgown, slippers and thick plaid shawl. Her nose was a little on the red side, but it often has that tendency.

'All those germs,' my mother said defiantly. 'From all those strange people.'

'Hello, sis,' Ivy said, ignoring her and giving me a peck on the cheek. 'You look well. How are you getting on with Father in the stables? Sounds rather a rum do to me.'

Ma pounced. 'Not nearly as rum as going up and down the road all day on an omnibus.' She pronounced the word with great distaste. 'It's a wonder you don't get dizzy and fall off! You'll have broken bones soon, along with pneumonia. Can't you talk some sense into your sister, Grace? She won't listen to me.'

Ivy sighed and raised her eyebrows at me. I could imagine exactly how she felt; Mother had probably been going on at her ever since she'd arrived. No wonder she'd decided on an early night.

'Leave it for now, eh, Ma?' I said. 'Listen to this.' My news would take her mind off Ivy's omnibus. Not the fact that I'd been dismissed, which I'd decided to try and keep secret from my mother for as long as possible (she was bound to say, 'Didn't I tell you working in the stables was a mistake?'), but the plans to turn Swallowcliffe into a home for wounded officers, and the Vyes going off to America. Ma hadn't been up at the Hall that day so this would be the first she'd heard of it.

'That's one way of riding out the war, I suppose,' Ivy remarked when I'd finished. 'Do you think they're hoping to stay away till it's over?'

'How can you say such a thing?' Ma was outraged. 'Lord Vye's only doing what's best for Swallowcliffe; he has things on his mind that we can't possibly understand. I don't know, Ivy, you're so contrary these days. Why can't we get along like we used to?'

Ivy had got out of the habit of being at home, that's what it was. She'd forgotten nobody can say a word against Lord Vye in Ma's hearing; if His Lordship said black was white, she'd agree with him. The funny thing is, Ma can't bear Colonel Vye, even though he's part of the same family. Everything Lord Vye does is right, and everything his brother the Colonel does is wrong - that's what you have to remember when you're talking to our mother.

There was a fire burning in the front room, so Ma told Ivy and I to take our tea through there and have a chat while she finished cooking the mince pies (her pastry melts in your mouth, it's so light). I think she realised we needed a little time to ourselves. I sat on the hearthrug opposite Ivy with my back against a chair, watching the flames leap and flicker, while she told me about her new life.

'It's such fun, Gracie! I can't tell you. When I heard a rumour they were looking for girls to fill in on the buses for the men going off to war, I jumped at the chance. I knew I'd love it, and I do. You can have a chat with the passengers, and we do get all sorts, Ma's right. Such interesting people, sometimes! There's the odd awkward customer now and then, but I can give as good as I get.'

She broke off to blow her nose, then tucked the hankie back in her dressing-gown pocket. 'We had ever such a grand lady waiting for the number 19 last week - Ma would have been delighted. All dressed up in furs, she was, and you could tell she'd never set foot in an omnibus before. There was a girl with her, about your age, and she was pretty wet behind the ears as well. Goodness knows why they'd decided to take the bus and not a hansom cab. Perhaps it was their war effort, mixing with the lower classes and all that. Anyway, we drew up at the stop and the girl jumped on first with the duchess following behind. She waited for me to help her up on the platform - probably expected me to curtsey, into the bargain - but then she got herself into a terrible flap. Started thumping with her stick to call the girl back, and you'll never guess why. She said - ' and here Ivy put on a quavery high-pitched voice, "'Gwendolen! Come here! We must get awff this omnibus immediately." The girl said, "But why, Great Aunt? It'll take us to Chelsea." "So it may," said the duchess, "but it's simply full of people we don't know."'

I laughed so hard my stomach ached. You can say this much for Ivy - she can tell a good story. She was chuckling too, but then her face grew serious as she stared into the glowing heart of the fire, sipping her tea.

'I'm never going back into service when the war's over,' she told me. 'I couldn't, not now. It might be better for you, working with Father in the stables, but I'm not fetching and carrying or bowing and scraping to a mistress after this. I want a life of my own, not the leftovers of somebody else's.'

'Well, as a matter of fact - ' I began, about to explain what had happened to me that afternoon, when suddenly Ma rushed into the room and stopped me in mid-sentence.

'Grace, your father's outside. He needs you. Quickly! Here's your coat.'

What on earth could be the trouble? Da knew I wasn't allowed anywhere near the horses now. I'd had to tell him about being given my marching orders; we'd had a long, sad talk about it in the harness room before I came home, with a good few tears on my part, I have to admit. To have found a job that made me so happy, only to have it snatched away, seemed very cruel.

I hurried outside, to find my father waiting with Moonlight and the gig by the gates. 'What is it?' I asked, while Ma went to open them. 'How can I come with you after what Mr Gallagher said? He'll have my guts for garters.'

'Never mind about that,' he replied. 'This is an emergency. I may need you to hold the horse or drive the Vyes home while I stay behind, and Mr Gallagher will just have to put up with it. There's been an accident. Quickly now, Grace - don't waste any more time.'

It was a while before Da came home again, in the early hours of a raw, frosty morning. I was already up at the stables putting Moonlight away, having taken Lord and Lady Vye back in the gig as he'd predicted. No one had been hurt in the accident, thank goodness, but Mr Gallagher had driven the Rolls-Royce into a ditch on the way back from their dinner party, and there it was firmly stuck. Luckily there had been a public house with a telephone not far away, so they were able to call for help. Her Ladyship was quite shaken, and Lord Vye was spitting tacks.

'The man was blind drunk,' he muttered, climbing up into the gig in his immaculate dinner jacket and white bow tie. 'The cheek of it, helping himself to port in the butler's pantry while we were having dinner! He could have killed us all. And goodness knows how much the motor will cost to repair.'

'William will sort everything out,' Lady Vye said. 'I only hope he won't have to wait too long for the policeman to arrive. Thank you both so much for rescuing us, Grace.'

'It's a pleasure, M'lady.' And so it was. I'd have driven the gig twenty miles through a snowstorm to see the back of Mr Gallagher, weaving unsteadily down the road towards the pub. Lord Vye had given him five shillings to cover the cost of a room for the night, and sent him packing to sleep it off. 'He's lucky to get that, the scoundrel! If he ever shows his face at the Hall again, I shall have him arrested. Dash it all, how are we to manage without the motor-car over Christmas? I've offered Freddy Warburton a lift to the golf club tomorrow. He won't appreciate having to ride in a dog-cart.'

Well, as it turned out, the Rolls was back in the barn before His Lordship woke up next morning.

Da and the policeman had managed to push it out of the ditch and discovered that the damage consisted of a smashed headlamp, a dented front wing, and a long scratch in the paintwork along one side. The motor-car could still be driven, so my father drove it home. I couldn't believe my ears when I heard the sound of the engine, and looked out of the harness-room window to see the Rolls-Royce sailing past with Da sitting in the driving seat as though he'd been born to it. He tooted on the horn for me to open the barn doors.

'This driving business isn't so difficult if you take it slowly,' he said, steering the motor carefully inside.

The next day, he drove Lord Vye and Mr Warburton to the golf club, having arranged to take the Rolls-Royce into the mechanic's after Christmas, while I looked after the stables. His Lordship declared my father would benefit from a few more driving lessons, but he seemed to be a safe pair of hands and at least he could stay on the road. Mr Gallagher had gone, I had my job back, my parents could stay in the gate lodge and Tom was coming home; if it wasn't for the war, everything would have been perfect. The thought of what my brother was about to face hung over us like a dark, heavy cloud. This war was meant to have been over by Christmas, that's what people had said, but there was no sign of it ending any time soon. Our boys were sitting in their trenches, the Germans were stuck in theirs - how was the stalemate ever going to be broken?

Da and I were giving the horses their mid-morning feed on Christmas Eve when we had a couple of visitors in the stables: Colonel Vye and Philip Hathaway. I hadn't seen the Colonel since he'd sent me packing down the hill that time in the summer and shrank back inside Bealla's stall, hoping he wouldn't notice me now. Still, I knew he'd been out in France and a girl would have to be stony-hearted indeed not to feel glad he was safe for the time being. I assumed he wanted to talk to my father but, after they'd exchanged a few words, it was me he came to find. 'Grace, isn't it? I'm sorry I didn't recognise you the last time we met.'

'That's all right, sir. You had no reason to.' I'm not sure I would have picked him out in a crowd now. He looked as though he hadn't slept for a fortnight, and he must have lost about a stone in weight: his riding breeches were hanging off him.

'Sad news, I'm afraid,' he went on briskly, 'but I thought you ought to know. Copenhagen's gone, I'm very sorry to say. A shell went off next to us and he caught a fragment in the neck. Severed his artery, and there was nothing we could do. Still, at least it was all over quickly.'

'Oh,' I gasped, feeling a pain in my chest as though someone had hit me. 'Oh, I'm so sorry.'

'Yes, a very great shame.' He gave me a sad smile. 'He was a fine horse, one of the best. Always put his heart into the job, and the men loved him. Used to cheer them up just to see him, that's what they said. It's a jolly good thing I was able to take him out to France with me and I've you to thank for that, or so Philip tells me. One good turn deserves another, eh? Anything I can do for you, just let me know.'

'Yes, sir,' I said automatically.

He patted my arm. 'I don't think he suffered much, you know. And it was the way he would have wanted to go, in the thick of things. A hero's death, you might say.'

But I could think of nothing but the glorious ride we had shared, Copenhagen and I, racing over the lush Swallowcliffe turf with the wind in our faces and the sun beating down on us. What a waste! Such a beautiful, intelligent creature, killed in a second for no good reason at all. And then suddenly the terrible thought occurred to me that perhaps I'd played a part in Copenhagen's death. Maybe if he'd been taken away with the other horses, he wouldn't have ended up in such danger, having to gallop about near the enemy lines in a hail of shells and bullets. Colonel Vye was still talking, but I couldn't hear a word. Copenhagen might still be alive if I'd minded my own business. Whatever had possessed me to interfere?

'Grace?' My father was standing behind me. 'I'll take care of Bella. Run along and saddle up Moonlight for Master Philip.'

I went about my business automatically, although my fingers were trembling and it took me a while to get Moonlight ready. Trust Philip Hathaway to turn up, adding to my difficulties.

'It's not your fault, what happened,' he said quietly when I handed the horse over. 'Uncle Rory says if someone else had been riding Copenhagen when he was killed, it would have been a great deal harder to bear. They were together till the end, and that's down to you.'

But I only turned my head away, not wanting him to see me cry.

Chapter Eight

The French Riviera is now easily and comfortably reached from England via Dieppe by through trains with sleeping accommodation. A few hotels have been requisitioned by the military authorities for wounded soldiers, but only slight cases are sent as the Riviera is too far removed from the seat of war to allow of serious wounds or illness coming there. The Season 1914-1915 will be quiet and 'Germanless' - an old-fashioned 'Riviera season' with every sports, distraction, etc.
From *The Times*, 23 December 1914

CHRISTMAS WASN'T QUITE AS wonderful as Ma had hoped. How could it have been, with such dreadful news every day from the battlefields, and train after train pulling into London packed with wounded men? The thought was in all our minds that Tom might be one of them soon, if he came back at all, and I prayed in church on Christmas morning as I'd never prayed before. We had a fat pheasant in the oven that had run in front of the motor-car one day, with Ma's crispy roast potatoes and brussel sprouts, but there was plenty left over when we pushed our chairs back from the table after an awkward meal. The effort of not mentioning the war made us either silent (Da, Hannah and me) or inclined to gabble (Ma, Ivy and Tom). The next day Tom went back to barracks and, two weeks later, we had a postcard to say that he was leaving for France the next day. I don't want to say any more about that; it is too painful to remember. Da and I shut ourselves away in the stables, Hannah hurried back to Mrs Vye and the babies, and Ivy took up her life in London on the number 19 omnibus, despite Ma's best efforts to persuade her otherwise.

Up at the Hall, the farrier came a couple of times to check Cracker's foot and declared that she wouldn't be blemished once it had healed. Lady Vye suggested that perhaps she should be sold as she was a little on the small side for Master Charles, and she was bought in the end by a young lady with a lovely light hand; I watched them riding around the paddock and thought they would get along together very well. It was sad in some ways to see Cracker go, but probably the best thing for her and a relief to me. Meanwhile, preparations began for the Vyes' trip to America, which would coincide almost exactly with the arrival of our first wounded soldiers. Mrs Hathaway moved into one of the empty staff cottages so that she could be on hand to direct operations, and Philip came with her. Now I understood what he had meant about us seeing more of each other; he'd given up his medical degree for the time being to help his mother. At least he was doing something for the war effort, I suppose, and it would be company for Mrs Hathaway since her husband had gone to work in a field hospital in France.

Being rather out of the way of things over in the stables, at first I had to rely on Florrie and Dora for news - and Ma, too. Some of the village lads had been recruited to work in the kitchen garden, so now she was spending several mornings helping out in the house. Word had spread about the Hall being turned into a convalescent home and there were more volunteers than we could cope with. Lady Vye's knitting party were particularly anxious to do their bit; they had been set to sewing pyjamas for the patients.

'You should see what a dog's dinner they're making of it, too!' Ma tutted. 'Half the pattern pieces cut out the wrong way round, and legs joined on where sleeves should be. If it wasn't such a nuisance, you'd want to laugh. Mrs Paxton and I are having to unpick most of the seams and start again.'

There was a great deal of work to be done before Swallowcliffe would be ready for its new role.

Lady Vye had ordered that all the carpets should be rolled up and stored in the attic in case they were damaged, and most of the paintings and fine china put away too. A quantity of iron bedsteads and mattresses had started arriving from all over the county which were to be laid out in the ballroom, the dining room and the main drawing room. One of the guest bedrooms on the first floor was to be turned into a dining room for the family, which didn't please Florrie one little bit. 'How are Dora and I ever going to manage? We shall be rushed off our feet, taking trays all that way upstairs.' (Lord Vye had already dismissed the parlourmaids, to save money.) 'And what if there are guests to dinner? It'll be impossible!'

'The Vyes will be gone soon,' I told her, 'and I can't imagine Mrs Hathaway will have time for entertaining. Charles and Lionel are back to school tomorrow, so you'll only have old Lady Vye to worry about. She shouldn't be too much trouble.'

We were all beginning to realise how different life was about to become at the Hall, and it did seem strange that Lord Vye wouldn't be there to keep an eye on things. I think most of the household had mixed feelings as they stood on the front steps to wave our master and mistress off to the railway station. Da was taking them in the Rolls-Royce, along with His Lordship's valet and Her Ladyship's maid, while I followed on behind with the rest of their luggage crammed into the dog-cart and one of the village boys to help unload it.

You could tell Lady Vye didn't really want to go. She looked worried half to death, and spent so long giving Mrs Hathaway last-minute instructions that her husband practically had to drag her away. When you say goodbye to anyone these days, I thought, it's hard not to wonder whether you'll ever see them again. We'd had a letter from Tom the day before, and he was very much on my mind.

18 January 1915

Dear Ma and Da,

Well here I am in France after a very long journey with stoppages all the time. It was a rough crossing so we were heartily glad to get off the ship and on to dry land. The countryside around here is in a terrible state - ruined houses, shell holes and rubble all over the place. It has been raining heavens hard every day since we arrived and mud everywhere. We are presently fairly comfortable, bedding down in some abandoned buildings in a small village (I cannot tell you any more or this letter would never get through) and being trained some more to prepare us for the Front. Please send my love to the girls. I think about you all and the dear old place very often. Try not to worry about me because we are in the best of spirits here and looking forward

*to seeing some action. Excuse this short letter but
things are still in something of a muddle and as
you know I was never much of a one for writing.*

Hope this finds you well as it leaves me,

Tom Stanbury

*PS If you could send some more socks it would
be a great help as mine are all in holes and no one
to darn them for me. I shall have to learn to sew.
Won't that make you laugh when I come home!*

The next day, Mrs Hathaway came to see us in
the stables. She's what my father calls 'a bustler',
marching about as if to say she means business, so
you'd better sit up and pay attention. I'd met her a
few times before when she'd visited us at the gate
lodge and liked her very well. She has auburn hair
and kind blue eyes, and while she might be bossy, at
least you know where you stand.

'Well, Grace,' she said, looking me up and
down, 'are you cut from the same cloth as your
mother?'

'I'm not sure, ma'am,' I replied, wondering
what on earth she could possibly mean. 'I'm not
much of a one for housework or sewing.'

She laughed. 'Neither am I. What I should like

to know is, are you a useful sort of girl who can be relied upon not to lose her head in an emergency, and doesn't mind working over the odds if the need arises? And can you handle the dog-cart on your own?'

'Yes, ma'am,' I said, meaning the same answer to all three questions.

'Jolly good. I want you to help collect the soldiers at Hardingbridge station and bring them back here - the ones who can get about, that is. Now, William, I should like to talk to you about converting the Rolls-Royce into an ambulance.'

My father and I exchanged glances. This was going to be difficult. 'I'm sorry, Mrs Hathaway,' he began, 'but Lord Vye left instructions that the motor-car was to be kept locked up until he returned. In case of accidents.'

She shook her head. 'Out of the question. We can't possibly let something so useful rust away in the barn. Do you know, the Rolls-Royce company can fit an ambulance body on to the back of an ordinary motor-car? I've been finding out all about it. Don't worry, Lord Vye has given me authority to handle matters in his absence. I shall take full responsibility.'

So now we knew the shape of things. Our door had been open wide (wider than Lord Vye had probably ever intended), and Mrs Hathaway wasn't particular about who came through. There were even rumours going round that the Swallowcliffe convalescent home was going to receive ordinary soldiers from the ranks, as well as officers, though we weren't to shout too loudly about that as it was against conventions. I wondered what old Lady Vye must have thought about the hoi polloi tramping through her house. Florrie was hurrying along the corridor one day when she saw the old lady approaching, so she stood to one side with her eyes lowered (the Dragon Lady not liking to be looked at). Unfortunately one of the volunteer ladies happened to be following on behind who didn't know the rules.

'She said, all cheery, "Good afternoon, Lady Vye. Not so bad for the time of year, is it?"' Florrie told me afterwards. 'Anyone could have told her that was a mistake. The look the old lady gave her by way of a reply! I couldn't resist taking a peek. Poor Mrs Jarvis went as red as that bowl of tomato soup on my tray.'

Yet we'd been shut away from the outside world for too long; it was about time to let in some fresh air. Why shouldn't a few other people put those big empty rooms to good use or wander through the grounds? Especially men who'd been to hell and back so that we could carry on living in freedom and comfort.

19 February 1915

Dear People

I am writing this to you all as I think my news must be passed around but aren't I the lucky one, with letters from each of my sisters and mother too. I cannot tell you how much I look forward to hearing from you and it is the same for the other lads. Thinking of home helps us through the hard times.

Things are not too bad at the moment. We are getting used to the constant barrage of shells coming over, Jerry is certainly doing his best to stop us sleeping. But our company sergeant is a very decent chap and keeps us cheerful. We even manage to have a good old sing-song sometimes. Now Mother I don't know what you would think of the state of this dug-out because it is knee deep in water most of the time no matter how hard we try to pump it out. Last night a mouse fell off one of the boards at the top into a billycan of soup that we were heating up for supper! I don't mind mice but you should see the rats. Huge great blighters, they are - Father could harness them up to a carriage. No sign of the socks yet but thank you for sending them.

Well, time for sentry duty so I shall have to say goodbye. God willing, it won't be too long before I'm home again. We shall have a few stories to tell each other then! I hope those lucky fellows you are looking after up at the Hall aren't keeping you too busy.

Grace's Story

Best regards from your loving son and brother,

Tom Stanbury

The fellows we took in at the Hall might have been lucky in one respect - they were safely out of the fighting for a while - but that was about the extent of it. I had butterflies dancing in my stomach, waiting to meet the train at Hardingbridge station for the first time and wondering what kind of state our passengers would be in. One of the professional nurses was with me to help them on the journey back: a cheerful, fair-haired girl from London called Margaret.

'There's no need to look so worried,' she said, squeezing my arm. 'They won't bite, you know. Just take it slowly and try not to tip anybody out.'

We had two patients to collect, one poor soul with both his hands blown away and the other suffering from some sort of nervous trouble. The man's eyes were starting out of his head and he couldn't stop shaking. 'Shell shock,' Margaret whispered to me. She had to sit beside him in the dog-cart, holding his arm to keep him steady. His uniform was filthy, caked in solid mud up to the thigh, and he didn't smell any too good either. The other chap was in a slightly better state; they must have cleaned him up at the field hospital where his wounds had been dressed before he came to us.

It was a great shock to see those two men, although I was ashamed of my reaction and tried not to show it. They had come from the country where Tom was fighting now. Was he seeing the same dreadful sights that haunted their empty eyes? Would he be in the same state when we saw him again? Later, when I knew Margaret a little better, I asked her how she could bear it and still keep smiling: this constant stream of men with the most awful injuries, some of whom would be sent back to the battlefield as soon as they were deemed to have recovered.

'Pity won't do them any good,' she told me. 'That's not what they want. I'm not saying I don't cry sometimes - you wouldn't be human otherwise - but I'm careful to do it in private. These fellows need reminding how things used to be, how they used to be, before this nightmare started. I reckon a bit of flirting makes them feel better than any medicine, and Matron can go hang. Telling us we shouldn't get too familiar! What would she know about it, the old trout?'

Her words made sense to me, and I tried to bear them in mind; not so much the flirting (which I've never been any good at), but just talking normally instead of putting on an 'I'm so sorry for you,' kind of voice. I'd have done anything to help our patients, and we all felt the same. Mrs Jeakes and Florrie were in charge of cooking for everyone, along with Dora and two new scullery maids from the village, but I never once heard Florrie complain. She and Mrs Jeakes were making plain dishes now, with no frills - stews and cottage pies, and jam roly poly for pudding - but I think they got more pleasure out of feeding those men than the noblest duke Lord Vye had ever entertained. We had officers in one part of the house and soldiers in another, with separate rooms for eating and sleeping, so there was a fair amount of running up and down stairs and corridors.

I couldn't do much more for the patients than ferry them to and from the station as required. The gig and dog-cart weren't the only vehicles I could drive by now. Da thought it might be useful if I learnt how to handle the Rolls-Royce, to help him with errands on private roads around the estate sometimes. I could start it up (luckily it was the latest model with an electric ignition, instead of a starting handle), go forwards and backwards, and turn the corner. There wasn't much time for driving, though, since Mrs Hathaway had come up with an idea for helping the men.

'Do you think a few of them might be able to go out riding?' she asked us one day. 'The weather's warming up a bit and I think they'd enjoy getting out and about. Nothing too strenuous - just ambling along on Daffodil or Moonlight for an hour or so would do them the world of good. What d'you say, William?'

'Very well, Ma'am. They'll need somebody to go with them, but we should probably be able to manage that.'

'I'll lend you Philip,' she said. 'Some fresh air would do him good, too. He's working far too hard, though of course I'm glad of the help.'

The Hathaways' cottage was quite close to the estate yard so I'd sometimes bump into Philip on his way up to the house early in the morning, or coming back late at night. He seemed to spend all his time on the wards; you certainly couldn't accuse him of slacking, even though he might not have been doing his bit for the army. He'd always say hello and pass the time of day, and I was beginning to find him a good deal less annoying. He didn't seem to be nearly as cocky these days; perhaps a spot of hard work was turning him into a nicer person.

Spring crept up on us, and it seemed to me that Swallowcliffe had never looked so lovely. Our rose garden might have been turned over to growing vegetables, but the woods were full of bluebells and daffodils tossed their bright yellow heads in the wind. Silvery waves on the lake sparkled and danced in the sunshine, and the trees were bursting with blossom. Men might have been busy killing each other all over the world (for the war was being fought in countries like Russia and Turkey now, too), but the world kept on turning, and there was still beauty to be found in it. So we dragged some of the beds outside on to the terrace for the men to enjoy the fresh air, and those who could walk were encouraged to explore the grounds. It must have helped heal them, breathing in the peace of those quiet woods and fields.

Spending time with the horses was surely good for the men, too. Animals are very comforting: they never complain, or expect anything from you, or look shocked or disappointed - just go along their own sweet way. Old Daffodil was steady as a rock, so even the patients who'd lost an arm or part of a leg could take her out. If they didn't feel confident, my father would put her on a leading rein and ride alongside. To help them into the saddle, we fixed up another mounting block opposite the first. I'd hold the horse still in between the two and Philip would stand on the second block, ready to offer a hand if it was needed.

We got to know quite a few of the soldiers who came to the stables as the weeks went by, and I became more used to being with them. They didn't want fussing over or parading about (although the volunteer ladies were always squabbling about who should take them for outings), and I didn't ask about what they'd been through unless they mentioned it first. Hardly any of them ever did. Some wanted to chatter on about nothing in particular, as if they were trying to drown out darker voices inside their heads, while others scarcely opened their mouths. Perhaps they couldn't see the point of talking any more, or maybe they felt that once they started, they'd never stop. There was one thing they shared in common, though. They were all desperately sad. You could see it in the depths of their eyes, the trembling of their hands, the uncertainty of their footsteps. Any spark of joy in their hearts had been put out, and the only thing left behind was a deep well of misery.

The saddest of all was Private Gordon Patterson. He couldn't have been much more than nineteen, if that: a great ox of a country boy with stout legs planted on the ground and a neck as wide as his head. Inside that strong frame, though, his mind had given way completely. It was dreadful to see his staring eyes and the nervous tic which made his head jerk as if someone was pulling it on a string. Philip told me he had been the only one left alive from a trench under constant bombardment for twelve days; the soldiers who were supposed to relieve his section had all been killed. He wouldn't speak to Da and me, but he'd often come to the stables and sit there on a bale of straw in the corner, holding his head in his hands to keep it still. Maybe he liked the familiar smell of the place as much as I did; he might have worked with horses in the past, or lived on a farm. Gradually he started taking more of an interest in what we were doing, and one day he picked up a dandy brush and started grooming Pippin, our little Shetland who pulled the mowing machine. I held my breath, wondering if I should step in, but he was as gentle as if the pony had been made out of spun sugar. From then on, he would spend hours in Pippin's loose box, brushing her over and over again with long strokes and humming quietly under his breath. We became used to him being there and he was no trouble, really.

One fine April afternoon, Da went out for a ride on Bella with a captain from the Hussars who was getting over trench fever. I'd been polishing leather in the harness room for a good hour, so it would be a welcome change to sweep out the stalls while the horses were away. As soon as I walked into the stables, I could tell something was wrong. Oats and straw had been scattered all over the floor, and Cobweb (the only pony inside that day) was dashing about in his stall, kicking the back wall. The hairs on the back of my neck stood up, although I couldn't have said exactly why.

'Is anyone there?' I called, ashamed of the tremor in my voice.

Suddenly an arm snaked out of nowhere and wrapped itself around my neck. I found myself slammed up against the wall, staring into the most terrifying face I had ever seen. It was Private Gordon Patterson, far away in some private hell of his own. His eyes gleamed with madness and there were livid scratches all over his face, as though he had raked it with his fingernails. 'Thought you'd come creeping up and shoot us while we slept, did you?' he snarled at me. 'Well, you've got more than you bargained for! I know the sort of things you do, filthy Hun, and I'm going to do them to you first and see how you like it. So what have you got to say about that?'

I couldn't speak; he was throttling the life out of me. All I could do was gaze into his crazed, bloodshot eyes and pray that he would come to his senses. 'Not so cocky now, are you?' he hissed, his fingers around my neck. 'You'll start begging for mercy in a minute, like the stinking coward you are. What mercy did they get, those pals of mine you killed? Do you still hear them screaming? Because I do. Now it's your turn to start hollering, just like they did.'

His fingers tightened on my throat. The only sound I could make was a strangled, choking gasp. A red tide rose up in front of my eyes, the blood drummed in my ears, and I felt myself slipping away …

Chapter Nine

We hear it said by all the soldiers who have come back and have been able to take a day or two's covert shooting, that the war seems to have had a disastrous effect on their marksmanship. They are disposed to attribute it to a little natural 'jumpiness' of the nerves, after listening to the shells screeching and bursting around them for so many days.
From *Country Life*, 16 January 1915

I DON'T KNOW WHICH OF US heard the sound first, Private Patterson or me. Cutting through the roaring in my head came a clear, sweet whistle, to a tune we both knew well: 'It's a long way to Tipperary, a long way to go …'

Patterson's fingers relaxed a fraction around my neck. 'Who goes there?' he called. 'This is my watch.'

'Time to change over,' came the answer.

'Caught yourself a prisoner, old chap?'

'Spying on us, he was, and some blighter's run off with my bayonet.'

'Looks like he's surrendered, though. Better bring him back, don't you think?'

'No, no!' Patterson shouted, shaking his head violently. 'Got to kill him! Quick, before he does for us all.'

Suddenly his hands dropped away and I fell back, coughing and spluttering in relief. It didn't last long. Patterson had grabbed a pitchfork leaning against the wall and thrust it at my chest, skewering me like a butterfly on a pin. If I hadn't been wearing the thick leather stable apron, this story might have had a different ending.

'Run him through before he can squeal!'

The other man raised his voice. 'Can't do that, Private. It's against orders. You kill him and the sergeant'll have you.'

'Orders?' Patterson frowned. 'Got to obey orders, Tommy!'

'That's right, orders are orders. Anyone surrenders, we bring 'em back alive.'

'Got to obey orders,' Patterson muttered to himself. I could hear the hesitation in his voice. 'Orders are orders. Bring 'em back alive, that's what the sergeant says.'

He lowered the pitchfork. I didn't dare move, although my throat was on fire and it hurt to breathe.

Patterson stared at me doubtfully for a second, before somebody stepped between the two of us. I knew already who it was, having recognised the voice: Philip Hathaway. I'd never been so glad to see him in all my life.

Gently, he took Private Patterson by the elbow. 'Time to go home, old man.'

The soldier put a hand up to his head. 'I'm so tired,' he muttered. 'Can't seem to get any sleep these days. It's the nightmares, you know?'

'I know.' Philip started guiding him towards the door, one slow step at a time. 'Come along with me and we'll sort you out.'

I watched them go, still frozen with shock. Patterson's shoulders were slumped and his head hung down; he looked quite defeated. Philip reached out to take the pitchfork trailing from his hand.

I saw the private's fingers tighten around it. 'Take away my weapon, would you?' he growled. 'What kind of a fool do you think I am?' He shook off Philip's arm. 'You're in this together, the pair of you! I know your game.' He was shouting again now. 'You're going to take me away somewhere and do me in.'

Philip took a step back. 'Calm down, no one's going to hurt you.'

But Patterson followed, lunging at him with the pitchfork while he shouted wild threats. The air crackled with violence and rage, and fear made my stomach lurch. Even if I screamed for help, there was probably no one about to hear and it would only make Patterson panic even more. He was standing between us and the stable door, a seething hulk of fury. We were cornered, like rats in a trap.

Philip was being forced backwards towards me. Perhaps even then, he might have been able to talk Patterson round – except that suddenly he lost his footing on the uneven floor, staggered against a pillar and fell, sprawling helplessly at the man's feet.

'Now I've got you!' Private Patterson raised the pitchfork with both hands as Philip lay helpless, ready to bring it down and finish him off. For a second, I wondered whether to try throwing myself at Patterson's back and pounding him with my fists. He was so strong, though; I might distract him for a moment but he'd swat me away as easily as a fly. I stared frantically around for a weapon. There was nothing to hand, except for -

Well, it might work; anyway, there was no other option. Seizing the bucket, I drenched Patterson in a stream of cold water as he bent over Philip's body. With a bellow, he turned around to face me. I was utterly terrified, but somehow desperation and fear helped me think straight; quick as a flash, I nipped in closer and jammed the bucket over his head. He fumbled to tear the thing off with both hands, sending the pitchfork clattering to the ground. I scooped it up and ran for my life.

'Grace! Whatever's the matter?' My father and the captain were trotting into the yard at that very moment.

'Patterson's gone mad!' I gasped, clutching the fork against my heaving chest. 'He's in there with Philip. Hurry, Da!'

I ran up Bella and Moonlight's stirrups and tied them by their reins to rings in the yard. Then I waited for what seemed like a lifetime. Nothing on God's earth would have made me go back into the stables, even though I was worried to death about Philip. Perhaps that was why. I didn't want to see what might have happened to him. At long last, three people emerged: my father and the captain, half-dragging, half-carrying Private Patterson between them. They led him straight towards the house, Da only glancing over in my direction to make sure I was well out of the way. A few minutes later, Philip was standing in the stable doorway and I was running over to meet him, and then somehow his arms were around me and we were holding each other, and the wave of relief washing over me was so wonderful that I wanted to cry.

'It's all right,' he said, stroking my hair. 'Grace, you saved my life! How can I ever thank you?'

'But you saved mine to begin with, so we're even.'

Talking had broken the spell, though, and

suddenly I was hot with embarrassment. What were we doing, Philip and I, clutching each other like this where anyone could see us? The same thought must have occurred to him; he dropped his arms and we hurriedly stepped apart. I searched in my breeches pocket for a handkerchief, not wanting to meet his eyes. When I risked a quick look, he was rubbing his arm and gazing into the distance.

'Did he hurt you?' I asked.

Philip shook his head; I noticed he was blushing a little too. 'Not really. That cold water seemed to bring him to his senses.'

I tried to think of something else to say. 'He was always so quiet before. Do you know what brought this on?'

'The army want him back at the Front - we heard this morning. His mind might have been shot to pieces but he could hold a gun and see where to shoot, and that's all they seem to care about. Well, he'll be no use to them now, poor fellow.'

'What'll happen to him?'

'He'll go to a secure hospital for treatment, I hope.' Philip sighed. 'I should have seen this coming. We'll have to stop the patients riding, it's too much of a risk.'

'No, you won't! Not on my account, anyway. Look how they enjoy it, and the good it does them. Something like this won't ever happen again.'

'We'll make sure it doesn't. Your father and

I will have to stay with the men all the time, and you must come and find us if you think something's wrong.' He took my hand. 'Promise me you'll be careful for once, Grace. If you came to any harm, I'd never forgive myself.'

'All right, I promise.' I had to extricate my hand after a few seconds; he didn't seem to want to let it go. 'Better see to the horses and tidy the place up, I suppose,' I said eventually.

Philip insisted on sitting me down for a while before I started work, however, so after we'd put Bella and Moonlight away, we went to the harness-room where I managed to make a pot of tea - clumsy and flustered though I was. When our fingers touched as I passed him the cup, I almost dropped it. We sat there making awkward conversation about nothing in particular until my father arrived ten minutes later. He might have been surprised to find us together, but he didn't say so; perhaps he was too relieved I was safe to notice.

I left the two of them talking and slipped away to the stables, wanting to be quietly on my own to think. The ground had shifted under my feet. What had just passed between Philip and me? Could he really care for me in the way I imagined, or was it nothing more than that: my imagination running away with me? My heart was thumping and my palms were damp, and it was only partly down to Private Patterson.

'Would you mind telling me exactly what you think you're doing, young lady?' I couldn't remember ever seeing my mother so agitated. The veins in her neck stood out like rope and her face was flushed with anger. 'Acting the hussy with Master Philip, of all people!'

Ma had paid an unexpected visit to the stables early that morning, a couple of weeks after the incident with Private Patterson, only to discover Philip chatting to me while I groomed Bella. What was I meant to have done, told him to go away? 'But we were only talking!' I protested. 'Where's the harm in that?'

'Where's the harm?' she repeated, taking me by the shoulders. I could feel her fingernails digging into my skin. 'I'll tell you where's the harm! Carry on simpering at Master Philip like that and you'll end up in trouble. What do you think he wants from you? Lessons in stable management?'

'You've got it all wrong!' My face must have been as red as hers by now. 'We're friends, the same as you and Mrs Hathaway. And I wasn't simpering. He passed me the hoof-pick and I thanked him, that was all.'

'Oh, Grace. You silly little thing.' My mother sank into a chair and put her head in her hands. By the time she'd straightened up, her voice was a little calmer. 'You can't be friends with Philip Hathaway. What could the pair of you have in common? I might chat with Miss Harriet sometimes' (which is what she still calls Mrs Hathaway) 'but that's quite another matter. I'm careful not to overstep the mark, and I've known her twenty-five years. Master Philip is a young man and you're a good-looking girl, even if you are dressed up like a stable-boy half the time. I know exactly why he's hanging around here, and don't you go getting any daft ideas about it.'

'It's nothing like that, Ma.' I hated the way she was making me feel: dirty and cheap. 'We talk about the war, and the patients, and books we've read. He likes Charles Dickens as much as you do! He's Tom's friend - why shouldn't he be mine, too? We're not so very different at the end of the day, even if he is one of the family.'

Philip had taken to dropping in on me every so often. We never spoke about what had happened after Private Patterson had been taken away and things gradually became more comfortable between us, which was a relief. I didn't enjoy feeling so awkward. True, my heart would usually skip a beat at the sight of him, but only because I couldn't help remembering the shelter of his arms, the comforting warmth of his woollen jersey and the feel of his heart underneath it, beating next to mine. I knew he had only held me because we had both been so frightened, and that such an extraordinary moment would never come again. No, I enjoyed his company and that was all. Da seemed to be out most of the time, running errands for Mrs Hathaway or taking the men riding, and I didn't like working on my own in the stables nearly so much these days. Philip seemed interested in my opinion, and we ended up having all sorts of conversations. I was glad now that I'd stayed on at school till I was fourteen - Ma had insisted on it - and that she'd encouraged me to read so many books. Philip and I still couldn't agree about the war, though.

'You should hear the men's stories!' he would say, trying to convince me. 'Being ordered to run straight into enemy fire, knowing they're about to be mown down. What's the point of it? It's just a senseless slaughter, and I don't want any part of it.'

'You can't help being a part of it,' I'd retort. 'We have to stick up for what's right and that means fighting, whether you like it or not. How does it make you feel, seeing these men wounded for your sake?'

We went round and round in circles, although at least we could discuss the matter now. How could I explain to Ma that Philip seemed to have become a person I could talk to about anything? I didn't even understand it myself.

'You haven't been listening to a word I've been saying, have you?' she demanded. 'All right, I'll tell you a story. When I was about your age, I had a friend called Iris. Iris Baker. She was the loveliest girl, quite a bit older than me, with hair yellow as butter and the sort of skin they call peaches and cream. She took me under her wing when I first came to Swallowcliffe, which was just like her: you couldn't find a sweeter, kinder person in the whole world. Well, Iris became fond of a young gentleman, one of the gentry. They probably talked about everything, too, only that didn't do Iris much good when she ended up expecting his baby. He dropped her pretty quickly then, her young man, and she died in the workhouse less than a year later. So you might like to bear Iris in mind the next time Master Philip comes calling.'

She got up. 'If I see the pair of you together like that again, I shall tell your father you're not to work in the stables any more. It's not right, and I've said as much all along. You'll have to come back inside the house. If Mrs Jeakes won't take you, I'm sure Mrs Maroney could do with the help.'

Now she'd got my attention. I knew Da had been worried about me since the episode with Private Patterson; it wouldn't take much to persuade him I'd be better off as a housemaid. My mother was quite wrong about Philip and me, but she could still put her foot down and make my life unbearable. Perhaps we would have to see less of each other - for the time being, at least. That shouldn't be so very hard.

'You've got nothing to worry about, Ma, I promise. But I'll take care not to find myself alone with him, if you like.'

She gave me a long look. 'You should have

remembered how to behave in the first place. Well, things should be getting back to normal next week, and not before time. His Lordship's coming home. He'll soon put a stop to this sort of carry on.'

We had been expecting the Vyes for weeks, but Easter had come and gone and they'd stayed in America. It seemed Lady Vye's family couldn't bear to let her go, but her sons must have missed her. They had to spend the school holiday with their aunt and uncle in London and that couldn't have been much fun, what with the Duchess of Clarebourne (Lord Vye's other sister, besides Mrs Hathaway) being so particular and not used to boys.

The day before the Vyes were due to return, we were all a little preoccupied. 'What do you think His Lordship's going to say when he sees what Mrs Hathaway's done to the Rolls-Royce?' I asked nobody in particular, pulling off my boots.

'Oh, Gracie, for the twentieth time – we don't know,' Florrie replied. 'And take those horrible things outside. They smell to high heaven.'

She was a little overwrought, because word had come that Alf had finally finished with training camp and was going into action overseas. I'd agreed to take her into Hardingbridge on my trip to the railway station the next morning (a Saturday), so that she could buy a few things to post him before he left. 'Now you won't forget, will you?' she said when I came back into our room, minus the boots. 'I'll call at the stables when we're done with breakfast, about nine. Promise you won't go without me, even if I'm a few minutes late. Grace? Are you listening?'

The Vyes' ship should already have docked in Liverpool by now and they'd be catching a train home the next morning. With so much else going on, why was Florrie getting herself in a state about a little bit of shopping? Then again, worry takes people in different ways. If I started thinking about Tom, I found myself sweeping the same patch of yard twenty times, or giving Cobweb twice as many oats as she should have had and Pippin none at all. Everybody was fearful for somebody they loved, and we were learning to make allowances for each other in such terrible times. Mrs Jeakes had lost a nephew at Gallipoli, and one dreadful day we learned that Isaac and Jim had been killed in the same battle, fighting side by side. That hit my father very hard.

'I remember the day I first set eyes on Jim, six years ago,' he told me. 'A skinny lad who wouldn't say boo to a goose, and about as much use around the stables to begin with as a yard of pump water. But he loved the horses, and you could see he was willing to learn. He had no family, you know. Isaac was like a brother to him.'

'At least they were together,' I said. Although how much consolation was that, really?

There was something I should very much have liked to talk to my father about. I'd found a letter in Da's coat pocket while looking for the key to the feed-store, and recognised Tom's handwriting. As soon as I started reading, I realised it wasn't meant for my eyes, and yet it was impossible to stop.

13 April 1915

Dear Father

Sorry not to have written for a while but to be honest I've been rather down in the dumps of late and don't want to worry Ma and the girls. So this letter is just for you – man to man, if you like.

I wonder what people are saying about the war at home. It seems a long time since we set off for France, all excited and certain we were doing the right thing. Well, are we, Da? Doing the right thing, I mean. Because I'm not so sure any more and that's a terrible thing to admit. You remember the ceasefire at Christmas that we read about in the newspaper? There's a chap I know who was out here at the time. He went over into no man's land and got talking to one of the Huns – a decent fellow, he said, who used to work at a baker's in London and knew the Walworth Road like the back of his hand. Anyway, this German said his lot were sick of the fighting and wanted to go home just as much as we did. What's the point of it, trying to kill all of them before they can kill us? And when will it end? When there's nobody left alive?

I don't want to trouble you, but these thoughts are going round and round in my head and it's hard to share them with anybody here since we're all in the same boat. No sense in rocking it, eh? But if anything should happen to me (which God forbid), I wanted you to know what was on my mind. You can tell people at home this war might not be quite how they imagine. I sometimes think about that girl who gave me a white feather and wonder what she would make of it.

This letter might not get past the authorities so I've asked a pal of mine going home on leave to post it to you at the Hall. Don't think too badly of me, Da. You've been the best father a fellow could have and all I hope is not to let you down. Remember how you used to race me about the yard in a wheelbarrow? I often find myself dreaming about the old days, and wake up happy.

Your loving son

Tom Stanbury

That letter made me cry, and it also made me think. If Tom thought the Germans weren't so different from us, of course he wouldn't want to kill them and of course he'd question the war - but where would that get him? Philip's idea of letting the generals fight it out with each other made some more sense to me now, and I ached to talk things over with him. I couldn't discuss Tom's letter with my father because I should never have read it in the first place, and Florrie was hardly the right person, with Alf about to leave for the Front. Philip was the only one I wanted to see, but he hadn't come by the stables for a few days and I could hardly go to look for him after my mother's warning. Why did she have to be so strict and wrong-headed? I went about my work in a very bad temper, and the thought that I might be missing Philip's company more than he was missing mine did nothing to improve my spirits.

Eventually I reasoned that Philip was bound to be spending more time with the family now, and I would just have to lump it. Apart from Lord and Lady Vye coming home, the Colonel had also arrived unexpectedly on leave; I'd seen him from a distance, chatting to Mrs Hathaway as they walked along the terrace together. He stopped to talk to some of the men, too, and didn't seem at all put out to find the house turned upside down. Yet what would His Lordship make of all these changes? Swallowcliffe had become a different place in the four months he'd been away. It even smelled different: carbolic soap and disinfectant instead of the usual mixture of beeswax polish, woodsmoke and flowers. There were nurses everywhere, patients in beds all over the house, Matron installed in the library, the billiard room full of medical supplies - not to mention the motor-car, with a great box fitted on the back to turn it into an ambulance. Every time I looked at it, I felt sick to my stomach.

'Stop daydreaming and look lively,' Da said, catching me leaning on the broom that Saturday morning. 'Old Lady Vye wants to pay some calls before the family arrive, so you'd better make sure the gig's spotless.'

'But what about going to the station?' I asked. 'I thought we had patients to collect.'

Da shook his head. 'Mrs Hathaway says there's nobody for us this week. They're all too badly injured and being sent to the London hospitals.'

I watched him drive the gig away half an hour later, wondering how I was going to tell Florrie the shopping trip she was so keen on would have to be postponed.

'Oh, Grace, sorry to make you wait.' She turned up all in a fluster, wearing her best linen suit and a hat I'd not seen before. 'I burnt the porridge and Mrs Jeakes made me scour the saucepan. I thought she'd never let me get away!'

When I broke the bad news, she didn't seem

to understand at first. I had to tell her twice, very slowly, and then she burst into tears. What on earth was going on? I'd never seen Florrie cry before, not even when she dropped a saucepan of boiling soup and scalded her arm so badly it came up in a blister.

'Don't take on so,' I soothed, patting her back. 'You never know, we might be going to the station tomorrow. It's not the end of the world. You can always post something on to Alf later, if the worst comes to the worst. We send things out to Tom the whole time.'

'Oh, that doesn't matter,' she snapped, shaking off my arm. 'Shopping was only an excuse.'

'An excuse for what?' I stared at her, wondering what on earth she could mean.

Florrie looked back at me, her eyes welling up again, and then out it came: the secret she must have been hugging to herself for weeks. 'Alf will be waiting for me at the church. We're meant to be getting married at ten o'clock! Now he'll think I've changed my mind.'

She clutched my hands between hers. 'Please, Grace, you have to help me get there somehow!'

Chapter Ten

It is rather a difficult time to get through, this period we have now entered, which a writer in one of the papers spoke of as being between 'the end of the beginning and the beginning of the end' of the war.
From *The Lady,* 11 February 1915

'WHY DIDN'T YOU TELL ME sooner, Florrie?' I asked, passing her my clean handkerchief. 'Why keep it such a big secret?'

'Because I can't risk Mrs Jeakes or anyone else finding out.' She blew her nose. 'I need to carry on working here while Alf's away. What am I going to do otherwise? Sit at home worrying and waiting for a telegram? I wanted to talk to you so many times, but Alf made me promise not to tell a soul. He's convinced his mother's going to hear of it. That's why we're going all the way to St Stephen's at

Hardingbridge. It was going to be just the two of us - and the vicar, of course. Alf's arranged it all. What if he thinks I don't want to marry him any more?'

I put an arm around her shoulders and wondered what to do. Father was off with Moonlight and the gig; Bella and Daffodil were out in the field and I could never catch either of them in time to harness up to the dog-cart. Anyway, Bella wasn't used to pulling a carriage and Daffodil was far too slow; it would take us hours to reach the town, if we managed to get there at all. There was only one possibility. It was such a dangerous, wild idea that I even succeeded in shocking myself, and dismissed it immediately. But then I thought about what a good friend Florrie had been to me, and how awful it would be if Alf got killed thinking she didn't want to marry him, and decided anything was worth a try.

'Dry your eyes,' I said, helping Florrie up. 'You're going to St Stephen's in style!'

My father had two different sets of livery. Top hat and tailcoat for driving a carriage; peaked cap, dark coat, rubber mackintosh (if it was wet) and goggles for taking out the Rolls-Royce. He kept the key to the motor-car in the inside pocket of this coat, which hung on a peg in the harness-room. 'Sorry, Da,' I told him silently, rifling guiltily through the pocket to find it, 'but this is an emergency.' With a bit of luck, he'd never find out. I slipped the mackintosh over my riding breeches and woollen jersey, tucked up my hair under the peaked cap and unhooked the goggles. We were set!

Could I really do this, though? Drive all that way without killing the pair of us or running the motor-car into a ditch, like Mr Gallagher?

Florrie didn't seem to have any doubts. 'Don't worry,' she said, giving me a quick hug. 'No one'll recognise you in that get-up. I won't forget this, Gracie. Now let's be on our way before somebody spots us!'

She must have been desperate even to think of stowing away in the Rolls-Royce - Florrie, this was, who'd never put a foot out of line in all the time I'd known her. She flung the barn doors wide, her face pale and her jaw set, and waited while I steered the ambulance through. (Luckily, Da had got into the habit of reversing it into place at night so he could drive straight out the next day.) Then she bolted the doors behind us, climbed in and hunkered down below the passenger seat in the place where people usually put their feet.

'Throw the rug over me,' she hissed. 'It'll look like your father's going to the station on his own as usual.'

You would never have known she was there. We'd have got away all right, for sure, if only someone hadn't been lurking in the stable yard, watching our every move. A certain someone who was waiting to step out and catch us red-handed. Mrs Jeakes was that certain someone. If we hadn't been going so slowly, I'd have knocked her over; as it was, I only just managed to stop in time.

'Now I've got you!' she cried, snatching away the rug to reveal Florrie's horrified face. 'I thought you were up to something, young lady. You've been a bag of nerves all morning. And what a surprise - here's Miss Stanbury, your partner in crime. I know it's you under those goggles, so you might as well take them off and tell me what you're up to. Going to meet a couple of young men, I suppose. The very idea, with Alf about to leave for the Front! And just wait till your father hears about this, Grace. Stealing Lord Vye's motor-car to go gallivanting! Well, I wouldn't have you back in the kitchen for love nor money, and I told your mother so the other day.'

'Please, Mrs Jeakes,' I interrupted when she paused to draw breath, 'it's not like that at all. Honestly.'

'Then what *is* it like?' she asked us, glaring at us both. Florrie had climbed out of the footwell and was slumped in the passenger seat, hardly daring to look at her. Coming face to face with the cook seemed to have drained her last drop of bravado. She glanced in my direction, begging me with her eyes not to give away the secret. I opened my mouth to speak, and then shut it again.

'I thought as much.' Without another word, Mrs Jeakes opened the passenger door for Florrie to step down.

'It's Alf we're going to meet, at the church in Hardingbridge,' I burst out, unable to hold my tongue a second longer. 'He and Florrie are meant to be getting married in an hour! My father took the gig so this was the only way we could think of getting there.' This plan was Florrie's last chance. Surely it was better to throw ourselves on Mrs Jeakes' mercy than admit defeat at the first fence?

'Oh, my good Lord,' she said faintly. 'Is this true, Florrie?'

Florrie nodded her head.

'Why didn't you say so before, you silly girl?'

'Because I thought you wouldn't let me go,' Florrie muttered. 'And I wanted to carry on working in the kitchens just the same afterwards, even if I was married.'

'Do you think I'm in a hurry to lose the best kitchenmaid I ever had?' Mrs Jeakes slammed the motor-car door shut. 'Now off you go, and look sharp about it. That young man has kept you waiting long enough - the pair of you should have been walking down the aisle months ago.'

'Alf's mother thinks he's too young to take a wife,' Florrie said. 'When he mentioned the idea, she had hysterics. We'll tell her when the war's over and she's not so worked up.'

I switched on the engine and revved the accelerator as a gentle reminder that perhaps we should be on our way. There wasn't a second to spare.

'Wait.' Florrie laid a hand on my arm. Heavens, now what was it? She turned to Mrs Jeakes. 'Won't you come to the church with us? You're the nearest thing to a mother I've got. I should like it very much if you could give me away.'

I'd never seen Mrs Jeakes lost for words before. She stood there, opening and closing her mouth like a fish, before eventually stammering, 'You'll have to let me fetch a hat.'

'There's no time for that,' I said, trying to keep calm.

'I'm sure the vicar won't mind,' Florrie said, moving up so there was room on the seat beside her.

Mrs Jeakes was still hesitating. Oh, when were ever going to leave? I couldn't stand much more of this shilly shallying about. 'I've never ridden in one of these things before,' she said, finally clambering up on to the running board. 'Grace, are you any better at driving than you are at cooking?'

'Yes, ma'am,' I replied, putting on the goggles and sounding more confident than I felt.

The engine stalled as it grated into first gear and Mrs Jeakes gave me one of her looks which I did my best to ignore. Inching past the front of the house was terrifying, but I reminded myself that no one could possibly recognise me in the cap and goggles, and felt braver.

'Can't we go a little faster?' Florrie pleaded, once we were on our way down the drive. Unfortunately my foot went down too hard on the accelerator so that the motor-car leapt forward in a great lurch, scattering a group of nurses walking up from the dower house. Florrie screamed blue murder and I saw Mrs Jeakes crossing herself out of the corner of my eye.

That was the moment I realised how horrible driving really was. Manoeuvring the ambulance around the yard was one thing; taking to the open road, quite another. I gripped the steering wheel so tightly my knuckles turned white and sat hunched up over it, trying to remember to look in the mirror now and then, change into the right gear and remember which pedal was which.

Once we were through the Swallowcliffe gates, I felt happier that no one would recognise me, but twice as nervous to be out on the public highway. At least there weren't many other carriages or motor-cars about, that was one blessing. If it hadn't been for that old man on a bicycle, everything would have been fine - and I still think it was only Florrie screaming and grabbing my arm as we were about to overtake that sent us swerving past so close. We didn't touch him, I'd swear it, but the bike wobbled and the old fellow flew over its handlebars into a ditch. We were within a hair's breadth of finishing up there, too; the motor-car's wheels were bouncing over tussocks of grass along the bumpy verge and I had to haul on the steering wheel as hard as ever I could to stay on the road.

'Is he all right?' I yelled, not daring to turn around.

'I think he's moving,' Florrie reported, looking back. 'Yes, he's alive! He's shaking his fist and shouting.'

'Oh, let me out!' Mrs Jeakes had her hands over her eyes. 'I can't do this, Florrie, not even for you.'

'We'll be fine,' I called, my heart thumping like billy-oh. What if I'd killed him? 'Just leave the driving to me. I'm getting the hang of it now.'

It was too late to turn back - but once Florrie was delivered and we were safe home (if we made it that far), I was never going to touch the motor again so long as I lived. Give me a horse and carriage any day of the week.

Brides are supposed to be late, and I got Florrie to the church only fifteen minutes after she was meant to have been there. Alf was already at the gate, looking out for her – very smart in his khaki uniform. You can imagine his face when the ambulance drew up and there were Mrs Jeakes and Florrie, sitting inside it. He opened the door and they spilled out.

'All right, love?' I heard him ask, lifting down his bride-to-be. 'You're white as a sheet!'

We all needed a minute to catch our breath. Mrs

Jeakes wiped her face with a handkerchief, muttering something I didn't catch, but she perked up once Alf had given her a nip of brandy from his hip flask. 'I was beginning to think you weren't coming,' he said to Florrie.

'We had a problem with the transport,' she said, 'as you can probably tell.'

'Just give me that flask, Alf,' Mrs Jeakes said. 'It'll take the rest of the bottle before I set foot in a motor-car again.' Tidying her hair, she untied her apron, rolled it up and thrust it at me. 'Now, isn't somebody meant to be getting married?'

'Come in with us?' Florrie asked me as an afterthought, but I wouldn't have felt right dressed in riding breeches and a mackintosh, and asked to be excused. I leaned against the Rolls and watched the three of them walk up the path to the church door, arm in arm. Tears came to my eyes, and I couldn't tell whether they were happy or sad. Then again, people always cry at weddings, don't they? That's another tradition. Even secret, last-minute weddings in the middle of wartime.

It didn't seem very long at all before the door opened again, and Florrie was walking through it as a married woman. I ran up to offer my congratulations and admire the ring, and then hurry Mrs Jeakes away because the sooner we set off, the sooner this nightmare would be over. Quite apart from the dreadful business of driving, I was terrified of my father coming back to the stables before us to find the Rolls-Royce gone.

'See you on Monday.' Florrie hugged us both, her eyes all shining and teary. 'Just think, I'm Mrs Fortescue now! Mrs Florence Fortescue. Doesn't that sound swanky? Oh, Grace, thank you for everything. I'm sorry about those things I said in the motor-car.'

'You get us home in one piece, that's all I ask,' Mrs Jeakes ordered, settling the travelling rug over her knees.

We set off. My legs were shaking at first but I kept telling myself to keep calm and, little by little, handling the motor-car did seem to become slightly easier. Once we were out of Hardingbridge, I noticed that Mrs Jeakes had opened her eyes and she only screamed once, at the sight of a herd of cows unexpectedly around the corner. I managed to put on the brake without stalling and we waited while they lumbered across the road from one field to another. Now that the engine was idling along, we could hear ourselves think.

'You were right, you know,' Mrs Jeakes said suddenly. 'You don't have the patience to work in a kitchen. I could never have turned you into another Florrie, no matter how hard I tried. You probably *are* better off in the stables than anywhere else.'

'I wish my mother understood,' I said, watching the lovely brown Jerseys amble past. 'She wants my life to be just the same as hers, but what's right for her is never going to suit me. We're chalk and cheese.'

Mrs Jeakes laughed. 'Oh no, you're not. Two peas in a pod, is more like it. And there's no need to give me that look. I first met your ma when she was younger than you are now, so I should know. She might have looked like butter wouldn't melt in her mouth, but the tricks she used to play! Sneaking out to meet your father at all hours, for one thing.'

'What, my mother? Are you sure?' Well, she certainly had no business calling *me* a hussy!

'Who do you think used to let her back in again? She wasn't so sensible then, you know. She'd jump into trouble feet first and only stop to think about it afterwards, just like you. Did she ever tell you about the time Miss Harriet - Mrs Hathaway, I mean - wasn't allowed to go to the fair, so your ma dressed her up in some old clothes and they ran off together?' Mrs Jeakes folded her hands in her lap and smiled infuriatingly. 'But I'd better not give away too many secrets.'

We sat quietly for a while before she went on, more seriously, 'I know why your mother wants you to follow in her shoes. You young ones don't understand how we feel about the Hall. We've spent our lives here - good lives they've been, too - and we want to see the old traditions kept going. There have been Vyes at Swallowcliffe for hundreds of years. Families like theirs make this country what it is and you're a lucky girl to work for them, so don't you

151

ever forget it.'

I decided not to take her up on that. Mrs Jeakes might be showing her softer side but I wasn't going to argue when she took on that tone of voice, and held my tongue as we carried on our way back to the Hall. When at last we reached the gates, she decided to walk up the drive instead of risk being caught in the motor-car with me - which wasn't very loyal, but I suppose her milk of human kindness had run out.

Mrs Jeakes must have had second sight. There was no sign of my father anywhere but Mrs Hathaway and Colonel Vye were waiting for me outside the barn, their faces like thunder. My heart sank to the very bottom of my boots. I drew the motor-car to a halt, switched off the engine and climbed down to face the music.

'I need taking to the station at Hardingbridge, Stanbury,' the Colonel rapped out. 'To catch the London train, so don't hang about, there's a good chap.'

For a second, I wondered whether to try passing myself off as my father. The Colonel was bound to recognise me sooner or later, though (especially if we had to talk) and it was probably better to come clean in front of Mrs Hathaway, who might speak up in my defence.

'Grace?' She stared in surprise as I took off the cap and goggles. 'I didn't know you could drive the ambulance.'

'Oh, for heaven's sake!' the Colonel exploded. 'Where's your father? I have to get to the station in time for the next train.'

'I think he's still out with the Dowager Lady Vye, sir.'

'Can you take me, then?' he demanded, bristling with impatience. 'Seeing as you seem to have commandeered this vehicle for your own use.'

I hesitated. 'The trouble is, sir, it's all right for me to drive about the estate but I shouldn't really go out on the public road, not being seventeen yet. If anyone should stop us -'

'This is an emergency, as I shall explain.' He wrenched open the passenger door before I could reach it and jumped in. 'If you can handle this motor-car, you can take me to the station. Come on, now, at the double!'

There was nothing else for it; I had to grit my teeth and set off on that dreadful journey all over again. I'd had some more practice by now, but Colonel Vye was a lot more impatient than my previous passengers and that made me even more nervous. (We passed Mrs Jeakes, trudging up the drive as we made our way down it; you can imagine her face when she saw us sailing past.) I knew the Colonel wanted me to hurry, but I wouldn't go any faster than twenty miles an hour; if we were stopped for breaking the speed limit, he'd certainly miss his train. Why did he need to get to London in such a hurry, though, when the Vyes were due back in a couple of hours? It must have been some urgent matter to do with the war.

At last we arrived at Hardingbridge station and Colonel Vye shot out of the motor like a bullet from a gun, pausing only to snatch up a copy of the latest newspaper and throw down a coin on the paper boy's stand. I'd have driven off straight away, except that a word the boy was shouting caught my attention. He was saying something about the *Lusitania* - a name I had only heard a few days before, when my father had told me this was the passenger ship bringing Lord and Lady Vye home from America.

Now it was my turn to leap out of the Rolls.

"'Ere, you can't read it for free!' the lad protested indignantly as I snatched a newspaper out of his hand and stared in disbelief at the front page. The world spun around me; all I could hold on to were these two dreadful words:

'*Lusitania* lost.'

Chapter Eleven

The great Cunard liner Lusitania was torpedoed by a German submarine off the south coast of Ireland yesterday afternoon and sunk. She was on a voyage from New York to Liverpool, and was with a few hours' steaming of her home port.
From *The Times,* 8 May 1915

IT WAS DREADFUL, not being able to do anything except wait for news. Shortly after I returned from the railway station, Mrs Hathaway called us all together in the chapel to explain what had happened, although nearly everyone knew by then. She said Colonel Vye was going to the Cunard offices (the company who owned the Lusitania) in London to see the latest list of survivors; he would telephone the Hall as soon as he had any information. The ship had gone down off the Irish coast, and survivors were being taken to the little port of Queenstown in

Ireland. In the meantime, she thought it best for us and the patients if we carried on working as usual, to keep our minds and hands busy. Mr Fenton led us in a prayer for the safe deliverance of our master and mistress, and we filed out again.

Mrs Hathaway had told my father about me driving the Colonel to the station because it was an emergency (he couldn't be angry with me, although I could tell he wasn't very happy about the idea) so it looked as though I wouldn't be getting into trouble for taking the motor-car after all. This was a stroke of luck, although it seemed wrong to have profited in any way from such a terrible event. I think we all felt guilty, to some extent: the ship had been torpedoed the previous afternoon and *none of us had known*. While I was taking off my boots and Florrie fretting about her trip to Hardingbridge, the Vyes might have been struggling for their lives in the sea or drowned several hours already. Of course there was nothing we could have done to help them, but it was uncomfortable to think about, all the same. The thing was, Colonel Vye and Mrs Hathaway had stayed up talking late into the night and asked for breakfast much later than usual on the Saturday. Mr Fenton had only had time to glance at the newspaper as he was taking it through to them at eleven.

After mid-day dinner, I went over to the kitchen to see if anyone was about and found my mother sitting with Mrs Jeakes at the big table. Ma looked upset, though she was trying to put a brave face on things. 'There's a good chance they'll be all right,' she was saying. 'His Lordship will have made sure they got into the lifeboat, and they can both swim.'

'So why haven't we heard by now?' Mrs Jeakes swirled the tea in her cup. 'Why haven't they wired, or telephoned? There must be a post office somewhere in Ireland.'

Ma caught sight of me and held up a warning hand; Mrs Jeakes was about to read the tea leaves. She turned the cup around three times with a great fanfare, clapped it upside down on the saucer, waited a few seconds, then lifted it up and peered in. 'Oh, that's not a good sign. Clouds everywhere, and a cross at the bottom. See this broken line?' She held the cup out to my mother. 'It means a journey with a sudden end.'

Not even Ma could think of a hopeful answer to that. I left them to it and went to look for Dora, whom I discovered closeted away with Bess, the still-room maid. There was nothing Bess liked better than an audience and Dora was perfect, being content to listen rather than talk. 'They must have had a guardian angel looking after them,' she was saying as I came in. Dora nodded sagely in agreement.

'Who do you mean?' I asked, my heart leaping with sudden hope. Could the Vyes have been found, and Bess with her sharp ears somehow the only one to have heard?

'Mr Thompson and Miss Merchant, of course,' she said (Lord Vye's valet and Her Ladyship's maid). 'Didn't you know? They were offered positions as butler and housekeeper for a rich American family, so they decided to get married and stay over there. Well, they'll be thanking their lucky stars now. We won't be seeing the Vyes again, I can feel it in my bones.'

That was more than enough gossip for me, so after I'd made Dora promise to come and tell me straight away if she picked up any real news from the servants' hall, I went back to work for the rest of that endless day. I couldn't get the thought of Lady Vye out of my mind. Selfish people were better at surviving; she'd help somebody else into the lifeboat rather than taking up a place herself. Somehow I wasn't quite so worried about His Lordship - a fact I'd never have shared with Ma. Isn't that dreadful? I'm ashamed to admit such a thing.

The afternoon dragged past. We were expecting Philip at three with one of the patients who wanted to go riding. One of the new batch of nurses came along too, a striking dark-haired girl with green eyes whom I hadn't seen before. I wanted to tell Philip how sorry we all were about his aunt and uncle, but she didn't give me a chance to speak, and almost elbowed me out of the way when I came to tighten Daffodil's girth. 'We can manage now. You might as well get on with your work.'

She and Philip went back to the house together and I returned to my chores in a thoroughly miserable mood. Dora came running in at tea-time and my heart turned over, but all she had to say was that the Colonel had decided to take a train up to Liverpool since there was so little information coming through to London. Every hour that went past made it seem less likely the Vyes were alive. It was impossible to imagine our world without them, or to contemplate Charles inheriting the title when he came of age. What sort of master would he make? Resting my head against Cobweb's neck, I decided to try and stop thinking for a while.

It was late when Dora came to the stables a second time. Da and I were giving the horses their last feed and preparing to close up for the night. As soon as I saw her stricken face in the lamplight, I dropped the bucket and rushed over. 'What is it? What's happened? Tell me, quickly!'

The news would have been hard for anyone to bring, let alone Dora. She was pale and trembling, biting her lip so as not to cry. I tried to help. 'They've found them?'

She nodded.

'Alive or dead?' There was no sense in beating about the bush.

But that Dora couldn't say, although she tried her best. 'L-L-Lady V-V-Vye - ' she began several times, until I was ready to explode from the effort of not interrupting.

'Is Her Ladyship alive?' I asked, holding Dora by the shoulders more tightly than I probably meant to.

She nodded, and I felt my whole body sag with relief. 'And Lord Vye, too?' I'd almost forgotten to ask.

But now Dora shook her head slowly from side to side. All I could do was stare in disbelief as she started crying in earnest. 'He's d-d-d-d-dead. Oh, G-G-Grace, isn't it awful?'

'I can't believe it,' Florrie said. 'He drowned, just like any ordinary person.'

'Well, he wasn't immortal.' I blew on my tea and took a sip, scalding my mouth in the process.

'I know,' Florrie sighed, 'but you'd have thought he'd be bound to get a place in the lifeboat. I suppose he gave it up for Her Ladyship - so he's a hero after all, even if he didn't have to fight to prove it.'

She'd come back with the dairy cart first thing on Monday, in time to help Mrs Jeakes with the breakfasts (our patients still needed feeding, even if none of the household felt like eating), and found me in the harness-room that afternoon. Alf had gone off with his regiment and the ring he'd given her was safely hidden on a chain around her neck.

Poor Florrie; the sinking of the *Lusitania* had rather taken the shine off her wedding weekend.

'How could those filthy Huns have done such a thing?' she asked again. 'Firing at a passenger ship? They say there's over a thousand dead, with little children and babies among them. It's an outrage! There were riots in Hardingbridge, you know - people smashed the window of a German baker's, and you can understand why. What Lady Vye must have been through! How did she look, Grace?'

'Like a different person. White as a sheet, and some sort of oil or grease in her hair. She was wearing an old skirt somebody must have given her, and no hat.'

Colonel Vye had taken the ferry over to Ireland to find Lady Vye, and had brought her back on the train the day before. Da and I had both gone to the railway station to meet them; he drove the ambulance while I took the dog-cart. Colonel Vye had wired to say a young lady was travelling with them and we thought it would be better if both of us came, in case there was luggage to collect as well. In fact Her Ladyship had only the clothes she stood up in, but the young lady chose to come back in the dog-cart with me so it wasn't a wasted journey. She was an American girl, a nurse on her way to work at a field hospital in France, and she and Lady Vye had ended up together in the water.

'Tell me again what you know,' Florrie asked,

wrapping her shawl more tightly around herself. 'Did that nurse really save Her Ladyship's life?'

'They looked after each other, from what I can gather. There was a door or some such floating past, so they held on to that for a while, and then a lifeboat took them in.'

Naturally I hadn't wanted to trouble Miss Jackson (Daisy Jackson, that was the name of the American girl) by asking her anything about what had happened, but it turned out she was desperate to talk. She sat beside me in the dog-cart and the whole dreadful story came pouring out: the sunny afternoon with a sea smooth as green glass, the sudden explosion that threw everyone off their feet, the shouting and milling about as passengers rushed up on deck or down to their cabins to find loved ones, the lurch of the ship keeling over, the launching of lifeboats, the panic and chaos and screaming, and then the shock when she leapt into the icy water, and the nightmare of people drowning in front of her eyes. She didn't say much about that, for which I was grateful.

'I hope you don't mind me telling you all this, Grace,' she said, putting her hand on my arm. 'But if I don't talk to somebody I shall go mad and you have such a kind face. Do you realise you're the first English person I've properly spoken to? I don't know a soul over here, so if Mrs Vye hadn't offered to let me stay for a while I'd have been up a gum tree. Do you think she has the room? I don't want to cause any trouble.'

I couldn't help but smile. 'There's plenty of room, Miss, don't you worry about that. And in fact, it's Lady Vye, not Mrs. I'm sure she doesn't mind, but you might as well know.'

'Oh, good heavens above.' Miss Jackson put her head in her hands. 'Trust me to get it wrong.'

I told her something about Swallowcliffe so she would know what to expect. 'I had no idea Mrs Vye was so grand,' she kept repeating, which shows you the sort of person Her Ladyship is: a real lady, for all that she's American and only one of the aristocracy by marriage.

Despite my preparation, Miss Jackson's eyes were like saucers when we trotted around a bend in the drive and she saw the Hall for the first time, laid out before us in all its glory. 'Oh, my holy godfathers,' she gasped. 'Now I know I'm dreaming. Imagine me, some nobody from New Jersey, staying in a place like this!'

'If you'd ever like a chat or a cup of tea, come around to the stables,' I offered, thinking she might feel more at home with us than the family. 'I'll show you where they are. Or maybe we could go for a ride when you're feeling up to it?'

I wanted to help her in any way I could. It was heartbreaking to see her broken fingernails and matted hair, and the web of cuts standing out livid against the pale skin of her arms. Mrs Maroney would make sure she was comfortable and had some decent clothes to wear, but I imagined she'd need a friend as much as anything. She told me they'd found the body of the girl she'd sailed over with; it was being shipped back to America to be buried. 'What can I say to her folks?' she asked, kneading a grey rag of a handkerchief in her lap. 'Mine have passed away so there's no one to worry about me, but she was an only child with both parents still alive. I should have been the one taken, not her.'

'But the fact is, you weren't,' I said, 'and you can't go on feeling guilty about that for ever.'

Who can tell why one person should live while another has to die? It has nothing to do with how hard you pray, or how brave you are, or how much anyone loves you. These days, all sorts of people are being killed every minute - men and women, rich and poor, good and bad, young and old. The only thing to do, I've decided, is to live your life as best you can and be jolly grateful for it.

The house sank into mourning while we waited for Lord Vye's body to come home; even the patients spoke in hushed voices. The blinds were drawn, everyone wore black and a new set of livery was ordered for my father and me, in preparation for the funeral. When would it take place? There had to be an inquest in Ireland first, which the Colonel was to attend. Why couldn't the body be released? The air hummed with whispered rumours and unanswered questions. Lady Vye kept to her bedroom while the Dragon Lady stalked the corridors with a face as grim as her black crêpe gown. Charles and Lionel had come back from school but they spent most of their time in the old schoolroom, or mooching about by the lake. There were no noisy games of cricket, no chases with barking dogs through the sculpture garden, no fencing matches with walking sticks in the hall. Everything was sombre, and quiet, and sad.

Daisy (that was what she had asked me to call her) came to the stables every day. 'I shouldn't be here at a time like this,' she kept fretting. 'If only there was something I could do! Lady Vye says not to think of trying to work until I'm stronger, but I can't bear hanging around the house all day when everyone else is so busy. I should be earning my keep.'

Now she'd had a few nights' decent sleep and a bath, she'd turned into a fresh-faced, pretty girl with hair shiny as a conker and clear hazel eyes, although anyone could tell she was still fragile. She'd lapse into silence every now and then, staring into the distance, and I could only wonder what dreadful scenes were being replayed in her mind. In the end, I suggested that she might like to help me cleaning harness in the afternoons, since she could sit at the table and it shouldn't be too taxing. It was nice to have the company and we got a good deal of work done, besides chatting.

She asked me about the horses who had been sent overseas - having noticed so many empty stalls - and my life at Swallowcliffe, and the Vye family; I made her tell me about America, and nursing, and whether she'd thought about spending the war with us rather than going on to France. After all, there were plenty of men to care for at Swallowcliffe and Daisy had surely seen enough danger to last her a lifetime. Selfishly, perhaps, I wanted her to stay. We were becoming firm friends even though she was a few years older than me. I loved the way she spoke, and the funny expressions she came out with, and the fact that she had such decided opinions about everything. (My other nursing friend Margaret would have liked her too, I was sure, but sadly she'd been transferred to one of the big London hospitals by now.)

'Oh, I don't want to outstay my welcome,' she said, smiling at the idea. 'Now, when are you going to show me those family portraits?'

Old Lady Vye had insisted that any paintings which could be easily moved should be taken down and stored in the billiard room in case they were damaged. Daisy seemed so interested in the family that I'd thought she might like to see them, and had asked the housemaids whether they might let us into the room one morning. There was a picture of the Vyes as children: Master Edward (who was to become our Lord Vye, God rest his soul), Master Rory (Colonel Vye), Miss Eugenie (the Duchess of Clarebourne) and Miss Harriet (Mrs Hathaway). The Dragon Lady was there too, unbelievably young but fierce already, with a toddler on her lap which was Mr John Vye.

'He's her only son by birth,' I explained to Daisy, lifting the painting out from its dust sheet. 'The others are her stepchildren, from the fifth Lord Vye's previous marriage.'

'It's very complicated,' Daisy said, gazing over my shoulder at the picture. 'But that baby sure is adorable! So the tallest boy with dark hair, he's Lord Vye who was lost with the ship?' She shivered. 'Gives you goosebumps.'

I knew what she meant. The children looked so innocent and carefree, but now Edward Vye was lying in a cold Irish mortuary while that angelic curly-haired toddler fought for dear life somewhere in France. Perhaps it was just as well they couldn't have seen into the future.

'There should be a portrait of our young Lady Vye here, too,' I said, wrapping up the picture and replacing it carefully in the stack. 'It was painted to mark her wedding to His Lordship. She's wearing a gown studded with pearls that was so heavy, two footmen had to help carry the train. That's why she's sitting down. His Lordship's there, too, but you hardly notice him. Yes! Here it is.'

Florrie and I had noticed this painting when Lady Vye had taken us on her tour of the Hall and one day, when the family was away, we'd crept out to the main staircase to have another look. I've never seen such a beautiful portrait, before or since. Lady Vye is dazzling in a pale gown with the Swallowcliffe diamonds around her neck; she shines out against the dark background like a full moon at night. Lord Vye stands behind in the shadows with one hand on her chair, looking slightly put out, as if he realises already that no one will pay him any attention.

'Isn't it wonderful?' I turned to Daisy - just in time to see her gasp and turn so white I thought she must be about to faint. Hastily putting the painting down, I helped her into a chair by the window and threw it open. 'Here, have some fresh air. How stupid of me, tiring you out like this!'

'No, don't worry,' she said unsteadily, her eyes still on the picture. 'I just came over dizzy for a second, that's all.' Then she looked at me as if she scarcely knew who I was. 'Perhaps we should go back now, if you don't mind. I've probably seen enough portraits for one day.'

It was strange, I thought afterwards, that she should have been staring at the figure of Lord Vye, rather than his wife, and that it was the sight of him which seemed to upset her so much. She had told me they'd never met on board ship; the Vyes always travelled first class while she had been in third.

What could he have meant to her? Nothing made any sense, and eventually I decided the whole thing had to be merely coincidence. Daisy must have been feeling ill already in the stuffy room and it was only my imagination that the picture had upset her.

I might have continued to think the same way, were it not for a conversation I happened to overhear shortly afterwards. Lady Vye was still not up to riding, but she wanted to see Bella so we'd brought the horse in from the paddock that morning. I was quietly brushing the tangles out of her tail when Lady Vye and the Colonel came into the stables. They were talking together in low voices and I shrank back so as not to intrude.

'Why should you think such a thing?' the Colonel was asking. 'The strain of these past few days must have been intolerable, of course, but -'

'Because I saw the body,' Lady Vye interrupted, her voice very clear and cold. 'It's bound to come out at the inquest, so you might as well know. You see, he didn't drown. There's a great deal more to it than that.'

Chapter Twelve

One always pictures Heaven, and I find myself apt to slip into an idea of a sanctified place, with harps and wings and things floating about ...But when you are struggling along through foot-deep sticky mud, and there are shells bursting on the path in front of you, and corpses lying about, then when you pray, you think of all the happiness and beauty you have ever known, and get a closer conception.

From a letter by Lieutenant Christian Carver from Flanders to his brother, August 1916. He died of his wounds in July, 1917, aged 20.

HIS LORDSHIP'S FUNERAL took place under a perfectly blue, early-summer sky. Colonel Vye, Mr Braithwaite and four of the senior menservants carried the coffin from its resting place in our chapel, out through the Hall's main doors and on to a farm wagon pulled by two young Friesian horses with black plumes nodding at their heads. They'd been borrowed for the occasion and only recently trained for carriage work. My father (who had to drive them) was worried they'd misbehave, but even they seemed to understand what a solemn affair this was and stood stock still while the coffin was loaded aboard.

It was a sad sight. Lord Vye had been the head of our household, for better or worse, our protector and provider for many years. A few of the servants had known him since he was a boy. Old Mrs Henderson was there amongst them; she'd been housekeeper at the Hall well before Mrs Maroney (during my mother's time, in fact) and, according to Ma, could remember the day Edward Vye had been born. The church bells had rung then to celebrate the arrival of an heir, and now they tolled to mourn his passing. His life had come full circle.

The family followed His Lordship's coffin. Both Lady Vyes came first, with Charles and Lionel behind, then Lord Vye's sister Eugenie, the Duchess of Clarebourne, with her husband and their two daughters, and then Dr and Mrs Hathaway and Philip, with Mr Vye's wife Henrietta next to him. (Unlike the doctor, John Vye hadn't been able to get back from France in time.) I caught my mother's eye as they passed, and knew exactly why she was looking at me so meaningfully. 'There goes Master Philip in the bosom of his family,' that's what she was saying, 'and here you are, in your rightful place.' I was waiting with the gig to take the Dragon Lady to church, since she'd refused to travel in any of the motor-cars kindly lent by the Duke of Clarebourne. The rest of the household was lined up on the steps opposite, but, all the same, it was clear where I belonged. My hair was tied up in a black net under a black top hat, and I felt hot and uncomfortable in my black crape costume with its long, cumbersome skirt.

The mournful procession of carriages and motor-cars set off at a snail's pace for Stonemartin church while the servants followed on foot. Everyone in the village had turned out to pay their last respects to His Lordship. Families stood at garden gates to watch the cortège pass by and then fall in behind; the children wide-eyed and quiet for once, their mothers ready to keep them in order with a warning pinch. Something was missing from the scene, though at first I couldn't work out what. Then suddenly it struck me. There wasn't a single young man to be seen - apart from Johnny Jones, that is, who was soft in the head and spent all his time throwing stones into the duckpond. They had all gone off to fight. What would become of the village if they never came back?

The only person who could have attended Lord Vye's funeral but chose not to, was Daisy Jackson. She kept to her little room (where the boys' nanny used to sleep), saying she didn't want to intrude on our grief. That didn't sound very convincing to me, and while it would have been cruel to ask too many questions, I desperately wanted to find out what she knew. Colonel Vye had returned from the inquest in Ireland very grim and quiet, but there was no news of any cause of death. And why had Lady Vye turned so cold? Her face might have been carved from white marble. It was strange, because everyone knew how tender-hearted she was; when her last horse had to be put down after a nasty fall, she'd wept for days. So far as we knew, she hadn't shed a single tear for her husband. 'Shock, that's what it is,' my mother decided, but I wasn't so sure.

After the church service, we trailed back to Swallowcliffe where Lord Vye was laid to rest in the family burial ground, beside the cedar grove in a quiet corner of the park. And that afternoon we were summoned to the chapel, for Her Ladyship to tell us what was going to happen next.

'We have all suffered a great blow,' she began, 'and I understand how unsettled you must be feeling. I'd like you to know that I intend to run the estate exactly as it has always been run until Charles comes of age. I shall have the support of Mr Braithwaite and Colonel Vye, who has managed to transfer himself to the War Office in London so that he can spend more time helping us here. There may be a few small changes, of course ...' and now she glanced at my mother, who was standing close by. I'd wondered why Ma seemed to be pushing herself forward; she still only worked mornings at Swallowcliffe, yet there she was, standing beside Mrs Jeakes like one of the regular staff. And incidentally, where was Mrs Maroney?

'Mrs Maroney has decided to return to her family in Newcastle,' Lady Vye went on, as if I'd asked the question out loud, 'but we're fortunate to have Mrs Stanbury, who will take over as housekeeper with immediate effect.'

Come again?

'There can be hardly anyone who knows the house as well as she does, so we shall be in good hands. Thank you, all of you, for your loyal support. Whatever the future brings, we will face it together.'

'Did you know about Ma becoming housekeeper?' I asked my father as we were saddling up the horses early that evening. It was such a relief to be out of the skirt and back in breeches again, with only a black armband for mourning. To be honest, I was looking forward to getting away from the house, too, and out into the open air.

'She only told me last night. Hey, girl, easy now.' Bella couldn't wait to get outside either; she was too impatient to accept the bit and tossed her head about until my father calmed her down with a quiet word. 'I think it'll be good for your mother,' Da went on, opening her mouth and slipping in the snaffle before she'd even realised what he was about. 'Take her mind off things.' We were desperately worried about Tom, not having heard from him for ages - too worried even to admit it to each other.

I was leading Moonlight into the yard when Philip walked up. 'There you are, Grace,' he said, almost offhand. 'I was hoping we could have a talk some time, when it's convenient.' It was hard to know how to reply after my mother's warning; I had to think for a second. 'We can talk now, if you like.' Strictly speaking, we weren't alone because my father would be following me into the yard any minute, so Ma couldn't really object. Had I done anything to offend Philip? He hadn't been near the stables for a while, and now he looked quite cross, glaring at me with his hands in his pockets. He'd changed out of his mourning clothes too, I happened to notice.

'But you're about to take the horses out. This can't be a good moment.'

'Why don't you come with us?' The words were out of my mouth before I'd properly thought about them, and for some reason I blushed. (Why couldn't I stop doing that?) 'It's a lovely day, and you could probably do with a break, after - well, after today.' Unfortunately now I'd started talking I couldn't seem to stop. 'I'm so sorry about your uncle,' I ended lamely.

'Thank you.' He looked at Moonlight as if trying to make up his mind. 'All right, then, I will.'

I handed him the horse's reins and ran to saddle up Daffodil, telling my father on the way that Master Philip would be coming for a ride too. He didn't seem to mind, and I thought how much more sensible he was about such matters than Ma; I suppose it was because he trusted me. At last the three of us trotted out of the yard with Bella leading the way, dancing about in excitement.

'This one wants to take off,' Da called, turning round to us. 'I'll let her go when we get to the gallops - she needs a good run. Don't worry about keeping up.'

So it looked as though Philip might get his private conversation after all. We rode along the edge of the park, past the woods where Copenhagen had taken off with me what seemed like a lifetime ago, and on towards the fields beyond. At the edge of the first was a broad stretch of grass, sloping gently uphill, where we would let the horses have their head. Almost as soon as my father had closed the gate after us, Bella was away, stretching her neck and throwing out her legs with the sheer joy of running free. Philip and I cantered along behind her for a while, but neither Moonlight nor Daffodil was in the mood for a race.

Eventually we reined them back and walked more sedately alongside the hawthorn hedge. I drank in the bitter-sweet scent of its creamy blossom, heavy on the evening air. Dusk would soon be falling and already the emerald green of grass and leaves had become deeper, more intense. A lark sang its heart out somewhere high above us, and a handful of swallows swooped across the empty indigo sky.

'Isn't it beautiful?' I turned to Philip, hoping the ride had made him a little less grumpy.

He wasn't looking at the countryside. 'Grace, I've been thinking things over,' he said, by way of a reply. 'It's my birthday tomorrow. I shall be nineteen.'

'Oh! Well, happy birthday for tomorrow.'

'Aren't you going to ask when I'm planning to join up? Come on, don't disappoint me. I was counting on a lecture from you about doing my duty.'

'You know what I think. It's up to you to decide.'

'Can't we talk it over one last time? You see, I'm beginning to come around to your way of thinking. I can't go on much longer, standing on the sidelines while other men are dying and being wounded, day after day. And I've been wondering whether there's another reason why I don't want to fight. Tell me honestly, do you think it's because I'm a coward?'

'I did at first.' I looked him straight in the eye. 'Not any more, though - not after what happened in the stables.'

'Oh, yes. That.' He laughed, but I shouldn't have brought the matter up; there was an awkwardness about the conversation now. Neither of us spoke for a minute or two, and then he said, 'It would probably take more courage to stay here than do what everyone expects. I still believe this war's wrong, and yet how can I speak out against it when so many men have been killed already? How could their families bear to think it was all for nothing? And yet that's what I feel - it *is* all for nothing, and somebody has to say so.'

The funny thing was, just as his attitude was changing, so was mine. I didn't entirely agree with him yet, but Tom's letter to my father and the effect of all our discussions had started me thinking rather differently about the war. 'Perhaps you should work in a hospital at the Front for a while,' I suggested. 'You wouldn't have to fight, but you could see how things are and you'd be a part of them.'

His face cleared. 'That's exactly what I was thinking. It would be a way of earning the right to an opinion, if you like.'

Daffodil was starting to fidget, tempted by the lush spring grass which I wouldn't let her eat. 'Shall we go back?' I said, turning for home. 'Da's probably reached the coast by now. He won't expect us to wait.'

'Just a minute.' Philip caught my arm. 'Grace, I couldn't imagine talking to anyone else like this. If I do go away, will you write to me?'

'What, me? Why?' I was so astonished, I simply couldn't think of anything else to say.

'Why not?' He smiled. 'I shall miss you, for one thing. You must have realised by now that I like you a great deal.'

My heart had begun pounding. Perhaps I had some idea, but I didn't know for sure. Now was the time to find out. 'What is it about me that you like, exactly?' I asked, my mother's words coming back to me. 'Compared to, say, somebody more suitable - like Miss Wainwright, for example.'

Amelia Wainwright was the daughter of one of the volunteer ladies, and spent a great deal of time up at the Hall with her mother. She had been the only useful person in the pyjama-making party, apparently; Ma was forever telling me how elegant Miss Wainwright was, and how neatly she sewed, and how prettily she spoke.

Philip groaned. 'Heaven preserve me from somebody suitable like Miss Wainwright! She's never had an original thought or done a brave thing in her life. You're worth ten of her, even if you are only a - ' He stopped.

'Even if I am only a servant?' I finished the sentence for him. At least he had the wit to look embarrassed. 'That's the point, though, isn't it? I'm a servant and you're one of the family, and if anyone finds out that I'm writing to you, I shall be the one in trouble. You shouldn't have asked me.'

'But don't you remember what we said last summer? When this war's over, everything will be different. Come on, Grace! When did you worry what other people think? Surely the only thing that matters is whether you're as fond of me as I am of you.'

'How can you possibly say that?' I snapped, angry that he should be so shortsighted and selfish. 'The world might be changing, but no doubt there'll still be Vyes at Swallowcliffe and servants to look after them for a good few years to come. I shan't be welcome in the drawing room yet a while.'

I kicked Daffodil on, suddenly wanting to reach the safety of the stables as soon as possible. It didn't matter how much I liked Philip, that only made things worse. We cantered for home, the words 'only a servant' keeping time in my head with the horse's hooves. Daffodil was so slow that there was no chance of leaving Philip behind, although I very much wanted to. He had made me realise the hopelessness of the situation far more effectively than my mother could ever have done, and I didn't want to be in his company a moment longer. At last I had to admit Ma was right: we couldn't even be friends, let alone anything more.

When we were dismounting in the stable yard, he tried to explain. 'Grace, I didn't mean to offend you, it was just a slip of the tongue. I never think of you as a servant.'

'Well, thank you for the compliment, but that's what I am, so you might as well face up to it. How do you imagine your family would feel if they found out I was writing to you?'

'Oh, my parents wouldn't mind in the slightest. They'd be glad - '

There was more to Philip's family than Dr and Mrs Hathaway, however. With perfect timing, old Lady Vye appeared to underline the point. 'Philip, your mother is looking for you.'

We turned around to find her standing there, leaning on the silver-topped cane she had taken to using outside. She must have seen us riding along together from her bedroom window on the eastern side of the Hall and come down immediately. 'Kindly return to the house at once. Leave your horse for the girl to deal with.'

He had to obey, of course. With only the briefest of glances at me, he was gone, and the Dragon Lady and I were left face to face.

'Get about your work,' she ordered me coldly, 'and stay away from my grandson.' She shot me a look of such intense dislike that I felt my insides turn to water. 'Don't imagine for a moment this is the end of the matter.'

I had no idea what was said to Philip, but the next morning I found a letter addressed to me, tucked among the brushes and curry combs in the harness-room where I would be sure to find it.

Dear Grace

I am writing to apologise most sincerely for any

embarrassment I may have caused you. Please forgive me - this was never my intention. Our friendship has been a source of great support to me, but I accept that it cannot continue. Rest assured that I will do nothing to compromise your position in any way.

With every good wish for your future happiness,

Philip Hathaway

So that was that. Ma would be pleased, at least. I didn't even wish Philip a happy birthday, and from that moment on, he no longer called by the stables for a chat. When he took the men riding, he only spoke to my father and scarcely glanced at me. Yet it wasn't quite the end of the affair, as the Dragon Lady had warned - although it didn't come to quite the conclusion she might have expected. I was summoned to see young Lady Vye in her husband's old study, which she had taken over as her own. Expecting to be given a severe dressing-down at least, or notice to leave at worst, you can imagine how nervous I was feeling. Her Ladyship had nothing of the sort in mind, however.

'Grace, I realise you're rather cut off in the stables,' she said. 'If for any reason you ever feel uncomfortable there, please come and tell me. I'm sure we could find something for you to do inside the house.'

'Oh, no! Thank you all the same, M'lady,' I assured her, 'but I should like to stay where I am.' Being with the horses was a great consolation, and the idea of working for my mother didn't fill me with any enthusiasm. I was very grateful to Lady Vye, however, for not having taken the same line as her mother-in-law.

Unfortunately now I would have to manage without Daisy's company in the stables. One afternoon she came to tell me that she had decided to begin nursing again, and would be helping out with the patients instead of cleaning harness with me. 'I'll still come visiting every so often - if you'll have me, that is. Will you, Grace?'

'Will I what?' I turned around from the window, having been listening with only half an ear. Philip was outside in the yard, chatting to my father, and the sight of him had distracted me for a moment.

Daisy smiled. 'You like that boy, don't you? I've seen the two of you talking together, so don't try and deny it.'

'Not particularly. Anyway, he's one of the family.'

'Why are you blushing, then?' she retorted. 'And does it really matter who his folks are?'

Naturally Daisy wouldn't understand - things were probably organised quite differently in America. Besides, she was in an odd, halfway sort of position at Swallowcliffe: not exactly a friend of the Vyes, but not one of their staff either. I tried to explain. 'It means we'll never be equal. Philip is Lord Vye's nephew. Even if I did like him, nothing could ever come of it.'

'Hah!' She gazed out of the window, narrowing her eyes. 'That sounds like a whole heap of baloney to me. The things I could tell you about your precious Lord Vye …'

'What could you tell me, Daisy?' I asked, trying not to sound too eager but hoping that at long last she was about to confide in me. 'Is it something to do with his death? There's some kind of mystery around that and I've a feeling you know what it is. Would it help to talk?'

She didn't speak for a moment, making me worry that I had pushed her too far. But then she said, 'Yes, I think it might. Keeping secrets has always been hard for me and this one is the worst. The thing is, Grace, will you promise never, ever to repeat what I'm about to tell you? Not to another living soul? I need your word. It can't become public knowledge - for Lady Vye's sake, not his.'

I promised faithfully. And so, at last, the whole extraordinary story came out.

Chapter Thirteen

The Lusitania sank about eighteen minutes - certainly not more than twenty - after she was struck. As she went down I saw a number of people jump from the topmost deck into the sea. One of them, I think, was a woman. I heard no screaming at the last, but a long, wailing, mournful, despairing, beseeching cry.

Dr Moore, American passenger on the ship, as quoted in *The Times*, 10 May, 1915

'I CAN'T BEGIN TO TELL YOU what it was really like, once we realised the ship was going down.' Daisy folded her arms and hunched forward over the table, looking past me to some faraway point in the distance. 'Most of the sailors were trapped below decks so there was hardly anyone to supervise the lifeboats. A few officers were trying to count the women and children in, but no one paid them much attention in all the panic and the boats were overloaded. My friend Esther got a seat in one. She shouted at me to jump in beside her, but there was no room and I could see the lifeboat was too full already. After it was launched, the lowering ropes broke halfway down and everybody spilled out. It was awful. People were being crushed against the side of the ship, and the boat landed straight on top of another one in the water. We saw it all from the deck, but there was nothing we could do.' Her voice trembled.

'You don't have to go on.' I leant across to take her hand. We were sitting opposite each other in the harness-room, with some tack and saddle soap between us as an excuse for work should anyone come in.

'No, I want to,' she said. 'You have to understand how it was.' She took a deep breath. 'There weren't enough life-preservers either, and people were rushing around trying to get hold of one. Some of them had started jumping straight into the sea when they saw what was happening to the lifeboats. After Esther had gone, I decided that was the only thing to do, so I started searching for a lifebelt myself. And that's when I saw him.'

'Lord Vye?'

She nodded. 'Although I had no idea then who he was. A man was trying to get his wife into a lifebelt next to me, and Lord Vye made his way over to them. That wasn't easy, because the deck tilted so sharply that no one could keep their feet and besides, it was slicked over with blood. He said to this couple, "You're putting that on upside down. Here, I'll show you."'

She paused again. 'So they gave him the life-preserver. But as soon he got his hands on the thing, he took it for himself.'

And she stared at me, willing me to understand the dreadful thing she had just said.

I couldn't, at first. 'Are you sure? It can't have been easy to see exactly what was happening. Or maybe he was going to give the lifebelt to Lady Vye, or some other person?' (Although that wasn't much of an excuse, admittedly.)

'No, it was for him. He started putting it on, just the same way as they had. The woman began screaming, and then her husband took a revolver out of his coat pocket. He shouted, "Give that back! I'm warning you, I'll shoot," but Lord Vye didn't take any notice. He just said, "Every man for himself, old chap," cool as a cucumber. But the man did shoot him, square in the head. He shot him dead, and took the lifebelt off his body and put it on his wife, exactly as it had been before, which must have been the right way up all along. I saw everything clearly.'

We sat there in silence for a while. I was quite lost for words. 'I shouldn't have told you,' Daisy said eventually. 'It was a mistake. I just can't bear to hear everyone go on about His Marvellous Lordship, knowing all the time the kind of man he was.'

Something in her voice made me ask, 'That's not the whole story, is it?' She hesitated, and I knew I was right. 'You're holding something back. What is it, Daisy? Please tell me.'

'All right, then, I will,' she said, looking at me with such anger in her eyes that I was frightened, though it couldn't have been directed at me. 'It wasn't the first time I'd come across him, your precious Lord Vye. I'd been out the night before to look at the stars, and there he was, leaning against the railings of the third-class deck. I didn't see him at first in the dark, but I could smell his cigar. Why should he have been there at all, when there was a much better view from first class? Because he was on the prowl, that's why - looking for some simple girl whose head would be turned by a few sweet words in a cut-glass accent.'

She shuddered, rubbing her arms. 'Well, he didn't find one. I had to fight him off in the end, but I managed to get away. He had his hand over my mouth and I bit it, good and hard.' She laughed bitterly. 'He wasn't half so charming then. And you know, when I saw him the next day, he didn't recognise me. I wasn't important enough for him even to remember my face. Maybe he never noticed it. I shall remember his, though, to my dying day.'

Now I wished I'd never asked; this final secret

was more than I wanted to know. Daisy could have told me the moon was made of green cheese and it would have been easier to believe. You see, I had grown up in the knowledge that if Lord Vye did a particular thing, then it was the right thing to do. This wasn't merely what we thought; it was one of the laws of our universe, an accepted fact. If Lord Vye cut my father's wages because there weren't so many horses to look after or carriages to drive, then that was only fair and must have been what all the gentry were doing. If he went off to America in the middle of the war, it wasn't up to us to question why he was going or wonder whether perhaps he should have stayed at home. That might sound ridiculous, but it was the way we had been brought up. To think of him acting in such a despicable way! It shook me to the core.

'How could that lovely woman have married him?' Daisy muttered. 'She deserves somebody ten times better.'

'Do you think Lady Vye knew what he'd done?' I asked, coming back to my senses. 'Not to you, I mean, but that business with the lifebelt.'

'She wasn't anywhere near him at the time - I never saw them together. But, you know, I always thought her attitude was kind of strange. I didn't even realise she was married at first. She only mentioned her husband when we were in the rescue boat on our way back to Queenstown, and then all she said was,

"Oh, Edward's very good at looking after himself."
Why wasn't she frantic to find him? He must have
abandoned her already, and she probably knew what
he was capable of.'

Daisy sighed. 'She'll have found out the whole
truth by now, of course. She was the one who
identified the body, so she'd have seen her husband
had been shot and must have suspected a scandal. I
suppose that's why Colonel Vye went along to the
inquest, to hush everything up.'

'What about the man who killed him? I mean,
he might have had a good reason, but it's still murder,
isn't it?'

'I think he died too, later on.' Daisy twisted her
fingers together. 'I saw his wife back in Ireland but
she was on her own, and you could see from her face
that she'd lost him. She'll have told the police what
happened, and they'll have told the inquest, and then
Colonel Vye will have told Her Ladyship. I'll bet my
bottom dollar it didn't come as any great surprise.'

It had to me. How could I have been so blind?
The stag's head above the fireplace looked down
at me with a very knowing expression. 'Surely you
understood how the game was played?' he seemed
to be saying. Well, now my eyes were open. I walked
out of that harness-room a very different girl from
the one who went in.

It was hard to see Ma's sad face whenever
His Lordship's name was mentioned and resist the

impulse to tell her what I knew, but I had given my word and couldn't go back on it. Daisy called by the stables pretty often over the next few weeks; I think she was worried about having confided in me and wanted to make sure I was all right. She had certainly upset me, there was no denying it. I was glad I'd never have to look Lord Vye in the face again - it's hard to take orders from a master you don't respect.

Daisy might just have been plain lonely, of course. She didn't seem to have made many new friends, and told me that the other girls kept themselves to themselves. 'Some of those volunteers seem to think they're too good to make beds and empty bedpans,' she complained, flopping down on the straw bale I was about to fork out. 'They look down on the girls who nurse to earn a living, and those girls look down on them in return because they're so useless. And I don't fit in anywhere, so nobody even bothers speaking to me.'

'Oh, take no notice of them,' I said. 'I know, why not come up on the roof tonight with Florrie and Dora and me? We'll have a good old gossip and forget our troubles. I'll come and find you, about half past ten.'

Ma had told me about this wonderful secret place. If you climb through the sash window in the corridor outside the housemaids' bedroom, you can walk along to a private corner of the flat roof, closed in by chimneys and the balustrade around it like a courtyard up in the sky. We often go out there on warm summer evenings to talk under the stars, keeping our voices low so we don't disturb anyone. (The housemaids don't like heights and leave the roof to us.)

'This is so cosy!' Daisy whispered, looking around. It was a cloudy night without much of a moon, so we'd brought our old candle lamps to light the way. Electricity might be a wonderful invention, but you can't carry it with you.

'K-k-keep your eyes open for Zeppelins,' Dora muttered. The Germans had started sending over these huge airships on bombing raids - like great silver sausages, they are - but they mainly head for London and only come when the skies are clear and there's plenty of moonlight. I was worried about Ivy, but she'd told us there was a cellar in her lodgings where she could take shelter. That was something.

'Isn't it dreadful about poor Mr Vye?' Florrie settled down with her back against a chimney stack. 'I saw him out on the terrace today in his wheelchair.'

Mr John Vye had come back from France, but he was in a sorry state. He'd been blown off his feet by a shell and had to have both legs amputated. Hannah told us the Vyes' house was a sad place now, and no wonder.

'That's the youngest brother, right?' Daisy asked. 'The one who's just had a baby? Poor man. Still, I suppose at least he's alive.'

'Old Lady Vye's taken it very hard,' Florrie said. 'We've been sending up food on a tray, but the plates come back untouched and she hasn't left her room. It's dreadful, and so soon after losing His Lordship, too.'

'Do you know my mother once saved Mr Vye's life, when he was a boy?' I told them, watching the candle flames flicker in the dark. 'It was a skating accident. He fell through the ice on the lake but she and Mrs Hathaway managed to pull him out in time.' I'd forgotten all about that until Da had reminded me; perhaps it explained why Ma had been so very upset to hear what had happened to him.

'Your ma sure is a part of this place,' Daisy said. 'Captain Chadwick says she could run it single-handed. He thinks she'd make a better job of the front line than most generals, too.'

'Who's C-C-Captain Ch-Chadwick?' Dora asked.

'Surely you've heard of him?' I said innocently. 'Everybody knows Captain Chadwick. He's the bravest officer in the whole of the infantry, and the handsomest, too. He has curly, light brown hair and the bluest eyes - Daisy, stop!'

She had thrown her shawl over my head, and now she was tickling me to try and stop the teasing. I knew all about Captain Chadwick, despite never having set eyes on him, because Daisy had been talking about him constantly for the past week. He'd come to the Hall with a bullet wound in his leg and needed help using crutches; help which she was only too happy to give. 'The way you're looking after him, he'll end up getting better too quickly if you're not careful,' I'd told her. Well, it was a treat to see somebody else blush for a change.

'Will you point him out to us tomorrow?' Florrie asked Daisy. 'He'll be at the sports, won't he?'

The next day, Mrs Hathaway and Colonel Vye were organising all kinds of races and a cricket match to encourage the men up on their feet - or their crutches, as the case might be. There would be separate races for the officers and men, but the cricket match was to be a mixture of everybody all together. I had the afternoon off from the stables to help, and we were all looking forward to a change in our routine.

'I suppose so,' Daisy said casually. 'I'm not really sure.'

Florrie winked at me, and the three of us burst out laughing again.

'Heard from Alf recently?' I asked her once we'd calmed down. 'How's he getting on?'

'Not too bad, I think. He talked about gas but they've got respirators now so they should be all right. Oh, I tell you what - the other day some of the lads went for a swim in this lake near their camp when suddenly the Huns started shelling them. They had to nip out of the water pretty quick and run back with only time to put their boots on! Alf said it was a regular beauty parade. You couldn't help but laugh.' Then she asked me, 'What about Tom? Any news?'

'He's too busy to write much.' I tried to keep my voice light.

'Don't worry. You'll get a lovely long letter some day soon.' Florrie squeezed my hand. There was no pulling the wool over her eyes.

The next day was a warm one. I took a back path to the south side of the house, not too unhappy for once to have swapped my heavy breeches for a cotton frock. Knots of people were scattered over the terrace and the lawn. At first glance, it might have been any other garden party at the Hall, until you looked more closely and saw the nurses' uniforms, the number of men on crutches or sitting in wheelchairs, the quantity of bandaged heads and limbs. Everyone was trying hard to enjoy themselves, but the laughter sounded forced to my ears. It all seemed a pale imitation of last summer, when the women had looked so beautiful in their frothy chiffon frocks and huge rose-trimmed hats, and none of us knew what real worry and suffering were. Then I saw Mr Vye in his wheelchair and pulled myself together. If he could manage a smile, so could I.

I made my way over to the long table at one edge of the terrace to join Florrie and Dora, noticing my mother talking to Lady Vye on the steps by the French windows. Why had I been so surprised to hear she'd been made housekeeper? Already it felt as though she'd had the position for years, and she was a darn sight better at it than Mrs Maroney.

Bess had told us why Mrs Maroney had really left. Apparently she had asked to see Lady Vye straight after Her Ladyship had come back from Ireland ('poor thing, in the state she was!') and declared that we couldn't be expected to cope with all these patients in the current circumstances (His Lordship being no longer head of the household, she meant), and that either the men went or she did.

'So Lady Vye thanked her very much and said she quite understood, and Mrs Maroney could have three months' wages and a decent character reference for her next position!'

Bess thought Her Ladyship had been wanting to get rid of Mrs M for ages, but Lord Vye had insisted on keeping her because she was so good at making economies. Well, now Lady Vye was taking up the reins at Swallowcliffe. It was strange: all the steel that had gone out of the Dragon Lady seemed to have been passed on to her. She even walked differently these days, very upright and purposeful in her sombre black frock, and she wasn't nearly so diffident about asking for things to be done. If there was something that would make the men's lives easier, she wouldn't take no for an answer.

I reported for duty at the tea table and was given a tray of glasses and drink to take out to the cricket pitch. Daisy fell in beside me as I walked across the grass, concentrating on trying not to spill the heavy jug which was full to the brim with lemonade and clinking ice cubes. 'Here, let me take that,' she said, lifting it off the tray.

'So where is he, then?' I asked. 'Where's your wonderful Captain Chadwick?'

'I'm not going to tell you if you'll only poke fun.' But she showed me all the same. He was third from the end in a row of officers on crutches, lining up to start a race - and he certainly *was* handsome, she was right about that. As soon as he caught sight of Daisy, he waved, and her face lit up. I suddenly realised she was looking happy for the first time since I'd met her.

'Let's watch,' she said, cradling the jug. It was just as well we did, because Captain Chadwick won by a head. He looked like the sort of person who was used to coming first, crutches or no, but very nice with it.

'Hard at work, Nurse Jackson?' said a sarcastic voice. The dark-haired girl I'd seen talking to Philip that day in the stable yard was strolling past, cocking an eyebrow in the most supercilious manner.

'Now *she* is the worst one of all for looking down on people,' Daisy whispered, glaring at her disappearing back. 'Lydia Lovell, that's her name.

Apparently her father has some manor house in the next village, and she lords it over all of us. What makes her think she can be so narky with me? She's about five years younger than I am, for a start, and she knows as much about nursing as a prairie dog. All she wants to do is sit by a man's bedside and look tragic.'

We watched Miss Lovell head into the distance, her white uniform dress pulled in tight around the waist and a nurse's cap perched neatly on her glossy hair. 'I'll tell you something else,' Daisy added. 'She's got her claws into Philip Hathaway. I've seen the way she cosies up to him, full of sweetness and light. You'd better look out, Grace.'

'It's got nothing to do with me. And thank you all the same, but I can manage now.'

I took back the jug rather too hastily; a little of the lemonade slopped over its brim. Daisy couldn't help not understanding the way things worked here, but sometimes it was irritating. How could I compete with some young lady who'd grown up in a manor house? Even if I wanted to ...

There was no escaping Miss Lovell. By the time I reached the cricket pitch, she was already there and deep in conversation with Philip. I should have been expecting to see him, but somehow it was a shock - maybe partly because he was wearing the white sweater he'd wrapped around my shoulders nearly a year before. That brought a few memories back.

Philip must have been waiting for his turn to bat and the two of them were sitting on the grass, a little way apart from the others. I poured some glasses and took them around to everyone else, hoping I could slip back to the house without being noticed. No such luck; Miss Lovell waved me over just as I was about to leave.

'What *is* the point in taking back a jug that's half full?' she asked me. Turning to Philip without even bothering to lower her voice, she added, 'I know it's hard to find decent staff these days, but *really* ...'

I was so angry and embarrassed that it must have made me clumsy. Somehow as I gave her the glass, my hand slipped and the lemonade ended up spilling all down her clean white front. She jumped up pretty quickly then, dabbing at herself with a handkerchief and spluttering with rage at me. 'Stupid girl! Look what you've done!'

'I'm so sorry, miss,' I said, leaving her to it. 'I seem to be all fingers and thumbs today.'

Still, I managed to hand Philip a glass without any accident (without meeting his eyes, either), then I picked up the tray and stalked off. My head was held high, but underneath I felt so wretched I could have cried. All of a sudden, I hated Swallowcliffe Hall and everything about it. I had no business complaining about anything at times like these, but occasionally being 'only a servant' was a little hard to take.

I ran into Ma on the way back. She must have guessed something had happened from the look on my face, because she drew me to one side. 'Don't upset yourself, Grace,' she said quietly. 'Just let things be. It's for the best.'

Perhaps she thought I was hurt to see Philip with Miss Lovell, although that didn't bother me in the slightest. His choice of friends was nothing to do with me, however badly it reflected on him. 'What do you mean?' I asked, avoiding her arm. 'I'm hot, that's all.'

'Perhaps you'd better go back to the stables, then.' She drew away from me. 'I think we can manage without you.'

The day had gone wrong, all right, but it was about to get a good deal worse. As I walked into the yard, my father came out of the harness-room to meet me. The door was open and behind him I could see a stranger sitting at the table; an unshaven man of about thirty or so, twisting a cap in his hands.

'Grace, hurry along and fetch your mother,' Da said.

'What, now? But she's busy - the sports aren't over yet.'

'Tell her to come here as soon as she can,' my father repeated, taking me by the shoulders and gripping them hard. 'This is important. It's about Tom.'

And something in his voice made me run.

Chapter Fourteen

*Full of wretchedness and suspense as the last few days have
been, I have enjoyed them. They have been intensely interesting.
They have been wonderfully inspiring. That they have been so
is due to the men with whom I have been. I always was an
optimist, I have never lost faith in human nature. Now I
know, now I know I was right.*

From a letter by Lieutenant John Allen to his family from
Gallipoli, 31 May 1915. He was killed six days later, aged 28.

'I KNOW YOUR TOMMY'S not a coward,' the man
said. (I never did find out his name; he was just
another private soldier from Tom's company, home
on leave.) 'I've seen him carry a pal half a mile under
fire, and it takes a brave man to do that. This officer's
got it in for him. He wants to make an example out
of your son to keep the rest of us on our toes, and
it's not right. That's why I looked you up, to tell you
what's happening. Tommy was always talking about

this place and my folks live in Kent so it wasn't too far to come.'

'Thank you very much,' my father said automatically.

'If the worst should happen,' the man went on, looking earnestly at him and Ma, their faces ashen, 'you mustn't ever feel ashamed of him. These generals snug at brigade headquarters with their bloomin' hampers from Harrods have no idea what it's like for us - sitting out there in some muddy ditch, waiting for a bomb to drop on your head or a bullet with your name on to wing its way over. It's the waiting that does you in, not knowing when it's going to come. Plays merry hell with any man's nerves, if you'll excuse my language.'

'What *is* the worst that could happen?' I was almost too frightened to ask.

The stranger hesitated for a moment. 'They've charged him with casting away arms in the presence of the enemy, and he'll be tried by court-martial. If he's found guilty, it's the death penalty.'

I felt a chill run through my body, as if every drop of blood in my veins had turned to iced water. The death penalty! Surely there must have been some mistake? Tom wasn't the type to cave in. What could have happened to him?

My mother buried her head in her hands. 'I'm sorry to upset you, ma'am,' the man said. 'That's how serious it is. He's allowed an officer to speak up for him, but I've come across the chap they've chosen and he's not up to much, truth be told. It's not right,' he repeated, shaking his head. 'Your Tom ought to have someone on his side with a bit of clout. I don't hold with the way he's being treated.'

He took up his cap to leave. Da shook his hand and thanked him again for coming in a flat, empty voice. Ma was crying now and my father put an arm around her shoulders, looking at her as if waiting to be told what to do next.

I walked the man out through the stable yard, this stranger who had appeared from another world and dropped a bombshell into ours. 'I wasn't sure whether to come or not,' he told me, his eyes troubled. 'But in the end I thought it was better you should know.'

Being in such a state, I almost forgot to thank him for his efforts, but I remembered my manners just in time and did so from the bottom of my heart. If this kind, decent man hadn't given up part of his precious leave to find us, we'd have had no idea what was happening to Tom until it was too late. (I couldn't bear to think that moment might have already come.)

As he raised his cap to bid me goodbye, he added, 'This is a grand old place. There might be someone in the family here who could pull a few strings for Tommy. That's how these things work, isn't it? And anything's worth a try.'

At that very moment, a picture flashed into my head of exactly the sort of person he meant. A man with connections high up in the army, who had once said that I should let him know if there was anything he could ever do for me. Well, there certainly was now.

Ma wouldn't hear of it. 'I'm not having you blabbing our business to anyone, least of all him,' she said vehemently. 'He wouldn't put himself out for us and there's nothing he could do anyway. Whatever trouble Tom's got himself into, we'll have to let the army sort it out in their own way. They won't listen to people like us.'

'They'll listen to Colonel Vye, though,' I protested. 'He's known Tom all his life and he's won the Victoria Cross. He's a hero! If he says Tom's being treated unfairly, they'll have to pay attention.'

'No!' My mother banged her fist on the table, sending a stirrup iron clattering to the ground. 'I'm not having Colonel Vye meddling in our family affairs. He's no hero in my eyes, and you're not to breathe a word of this business to him or anyone else. You know what people are like for gossip round here. I'm not having them saying Tom's a coward.'

I couldn't believe my ears. What did it matter what people said? Did that mean more to Ma than whether Tom lived or died? 'But –'

'That's enough, Grace,' Da interrupted, and I could tell from the tone of his voice that the conversation was over.

'This is nobody's business but ours.' My mother stood up, tidying her hair and her frock. 'I'm going back to work now, and I suggest you do the same. I'll pray for Tom and that's as much as we can do. If you tell a soul about this, Grace, I shall never forgive you.'

How could we possibly go about our duties as though everything was the same as usual? Horses pick up your mood in an instant, and Moonlight must have sensed my feelings from the way I was grooming him, although I tried to be gentle; he put his ears back and twitched away from my touch. I had to walk up and down the stable block a few times to try and calm down. Every instinct in my head screamed out that Ma was wrong. We couldn't stand back in the hope that things would turn out all right, because they weren't going to. Somehow Tom had got himself into the most dreadful trouble and we should have been moving heaven and earth to help him. What hope did we have, apart from Colonel Vye? I didn't know why my mother thought so little of him and just then, I didn't really care. I had never deliberately disobeyed her before but I would now, for Tom's sake; if she held that against me for the rest of my life, then so be it.

The only question was how? How could I get the Colonel on his own, to start with? I had hardly any contact with him. He spent most weekends at the Hall and would usually go out riding in the early evening with Her Ladyship or Mrs Hathaway, but my father always attended to him whenever he came to the stables. I would sometimes bring his horse round to the front of the house, but he'd be up in the saddle and away with only a brief nod to me. Well, somehow I'd have to contrive it, because Colonel Vye would be back up to London the next afternoon and I'd have lost my chance for another week. We didn't know when Tom's court-martial was to be held, but surely there wasn't a day to spare.

That evening, Bella and Moonlight were ready tacked up at six and I was ready, too, when the Colonel and Mrs Hathaway walked into the stable yard (she liked to use the mounting block, being on the stout side). If only my father wasn't hovering around so closely!

Da wouldn't go away, though; instead, he took Moonlight's reins from me. 'You can have ten minutes with Colonel Vye in the harness-room,' he said in a low voice. 'I'll keep Mrs Hathaway busy.' Then he gave me a slip of paper. 'This is the number of Tom's company, and the name of his commanding officer, and the place he's being held. That chap wrote it all out for me.'

I only had time to thank him with a look because here was the Colonel, very smart and soldierly in his chestnut leather riding boots. Now my courage nearly failed me. Did I really expect him to go all the way to France, just to speak up for my brother? He'd probably laugh in my face. Yet the thought of Tom alone in some field prison forced me to try.

Colonel Vye didn't laugh, but he certainly looked pretty surprised when I asked him for a private interview and told him the whole story - or at least, as much of it as we knew. 'I'm sure Tom's no coward,' I finished. 'There must be some terrible mistake. Please, Colonel Vye, I know it's probably too much to ask, but could you try and sort things out for us? You know how things are done in the army, and you could make sure Tom gets a fair hearing.'

I passed him the piece of paper with all the details on that my father had given me. Colonel Vye looked at it for what seemed a long time. Then he laid it down on the table and looked at me, scratching his head. 'It *is* a lot to ask,' he said, 'and I have to warn you - even if I did go, I'm not sure how much good it'd do. These courts-martial are often carried out pretty swiftly and it may be too late already for me to get to your brother in time, let alone gather any evidence that'll help him.' He hesitated for a moment, before adding, 'Casting away arms is a serious offence, and I can't believe he'd be accused for no reason. Have you thought about that?'

'I don't care what they say he's meant to have done. I know Tom better than anyone, and you couldn't find a braver, finer man in the whole world.

If they shoot him, they might as well shoot me too.' By now I was nearly crying, and down on my knees. 'Please, Colonel Vye, please won't you help us? We've no one else to ask.'

Gently, he helped me up. 'Of course I will, my dear, there's no need for all this. How long have I known your family? I seem to remember you putting yourself out for me in the past, besides, and one good turn deserves another. I just wanted you to realise that it'll be a long shot. I'll certainly try my hardest for your brother, but I may not succeed.'

He put the piece of paper in his pocket. I could have kissed him. In fact, I did - well, his hand, anyway. Ma would have had forty fits.

So it was back to the endless waiting. For the next few days, I went about my work as if in a trance. Tom was the last thing I thought about at night and first on my mind in the morning, and I dreamed about him endlessly in between. I knew it was the same for Da, too, although we didn't talk much. Perhaps he felt that he'd been disloyal to my mother, encouraging me to appeal to the Colonel, and didn't want to face up to what we'd done. It was the right thing, though, I kept telling myself. If Colonel Vye managed to save Tom, Ma would have to change her mind about him - and if he didn't, it wouldn't matter whether or not she found out that I'd asked for his help. Nothing would matter then.

Grace's Story

I wasn't tempted to share the secret with anyone else. Not Florrie, somehow, with Alf apparently getting along so well in France, and not Daisy, either, who only had room in her head for thoughts of Captain Chadwick. He'd been brought up not far from the Hall, it turned out; his father having been the vicar of a nearby village, and had promised to show Daisy his old home when he was quite better. 'He's lost both his parents, too, same as me,' she said, 'but their house is still standing. So it's almost like he's taking me to meet them, don't you think?'

'Almost,' I agreed, since that was the easiest thing to do.

It felt as though I was standing at the end of a long tunnel. I could see other people and hear them, but their voices seemed to come from very far away. Somehow I managed to keep hold of myself - until one afternoon, when Colonel Vye had been gone almost a week. My father had taken Bella out for a gallop, and the other horses were grazing in the paddock. I'd swept and hosed the stalls, washed down the gig, soaped and polished umpteen saddles and bridles, and then found myself sitting at the harness-room table with my fingernails digging so deep into the palms of my hands they'd drawn blood. My head was throbbing with the effort of not thinking and I knew that I had to get outside in a hurry or end up screaming.

Snatching up a hat, I ran out of the yard and through the gate towards the park; anywhere, really, just to escape. On and on across the grass, my feet pounding and my breath coming in ragged gasps, up the hill, a stitch in my side by now, until there were the woods ahead of me. Shaded, and cool, and quiet. I pressed my forehead against the papery bark of a silver birch, feeling the blood rush through my veins and my heart thump like a drum in my chest. What was Tom doing now? Was he listening to his own heartbeat too, and wondering about the moment it might stop for ever? I remembered all the times he had carried me on his back when I was a little girl, all the stories he had told me when I couldn't sleep, all the times he had let me tag along behind when it would have been easier to send me home, and then I gathered up every scrap of my love and sent it flying out to him, wherever he was.

Feeling somewhat calmer, I walked on up through the trees, not paying much attention to where my legs were taking me. The path wound around to that point where it opened out to give a view of the Hall - and there was Philip, sitting on a tree stump and looking down at the house. I'd have backed away, but a twig cracked underfoot and he turned around. Well, I didn't particularly care whether he saw me or not. All that business seemed very unimportant now.

'Sorry,' I said, a little out of breath still. 'I didn't

mean to disturb you.'

'No, I'm glad you did,' he replied. 'I've had enough of my own company. Won't you have a seat? It's more comfortable than you might think.' He got up from the stump and leaned against a tree trunk instead, his hands in his pockets. 'At least now we'll have the chance to say goodbye.'

'So you're going off to the war, then?' I sat down in his place, since it would have seemed rude not to.

'Yes. Not straight away, but soon. I'm to be an orderly in my father's hospital.'

'Good luck.' I couldn't help remembering the moment when he had asked me to write to him and, for a fleeting second, I surprised myself by wishing he would ask again. But why? Would my answer be any different this time?

'Thank you.' Of course, he didn't. I suppose he had Miss Lovell to send him news now, or Miss Wainwright, or any one of a hundred other ladylike girls who could write a much more elegant letter than me. Than I.

'Grace, is something the matter? You look very preoccupied. What is it?'

I should never have confided in Philip but, feeling the way I did then, it was impossible to resist. The whole story came spilling out. I told him what had happened to Tom, and the fact that Colonel Vye had gone out to France to try and help him, and even that my mother didn't want anyone else to hear of it.

'It's as though she's ashamed of him. Her own son!'

'Now come on, that's a little harsh. You can see why she wouldn't want people to talk. Do you think she loves him any less than you do?'

I had to admit that I didn't.

'Everybody deals with these things in their own way. Perhaps she just doesn't like asking anyone for help. And yet Uncle Rory is exactly the right person.'

'He's certainly been good to us.'

'Yes, I'm sure he would be. He's always been keen on fair play.' Philip sighed. 'I'm so sorry, Grace - you must be worried to death about Tom. For what it's worth, I can't imagine him ever letting anyone down if he could possibly help it. We used to get into twenty kinds of trouble when we were young and he always took the blame for me. I've never had a truer friend, before or since.'

I nodded, knowing the tears weren't far away, and stood up. 'I'd better be getting back. I hope everything goes all right for you in France.'

'Thank you. I hope things don't turn out too badly for your brother.'

I couldn't think what to do next and neither could he, I suppose, because we ended up shaking hands. Then I walked down the hill; quieter now, but somehow even sadder.

Grace's Story

Yet had I but known it, this torture of waiting had only one more night to run. The next morning, I came into the harness-room to find my father staring at a telegram on the table in front of him.

'I've been looking at this thing for ten minutes,' he said. 'Will you open it, Grace?'

Chapter Fifteen

I shall never look on warfare either as fine or sporting again. It reduces men to shivering beasts: there isn't a man who can stand shell-fire of the modern kind without getting the blues.
From a letter written by Lieutenant Gavin Greenwell from the Somme, August 1916

'YOU SHOULDN;T HAVE DONE IT,' my mother said. 'I told you this was our affair and nobody else's. Why didn't you listen to me instead of running off to Colonel Vye? Why does he have to go meddling in our private family business?'

'But didn't you see this?' I shook the telegram in front of her face. 'Tom's been acquitted! Surely nothing else matters except for that? Colonel Vye saved his life!'

'We don't know if it was that man's doing. We don't even know if he spoke up at his trial, this court-martial, or whatever it's called. Tom would probably have got off anyway and the Colonel need never have stuck his oar in. Trust him to try and claim the credit.'

Why did she have to be so stubborn and sour? Honestly, I could have shaken her till her teeth rattled. When Da and I had read the telegram from Colonel Vye, we'd thrown it up in the air and danced a jig together around the table, crying and laughing at the same time. Tom had been found innocent of the charge and, what was more, he was coming home! He'd been given a week's leave and the Colonel was bringing him back to us. Yet to look at Ma's scowling, suspicious face, you'd have thought he'd personally locked my brother up and thrown away the key.

'Colonel Vye went to France especially for us,' I said, deliberately slowly. 'He put himself to a great deal of trouble, not to mention danger, and even if he had nothing to do with Tom's trial - which I don't believe for one minute - we should thank him for that.'

'I'm not thanking him for anything. Don't you remember what I said, you naughty, disobedient girl? He was the last person you should have told.'

'He was the only person who could have helped us! Who else has friends in the army, or knows how to find their way around the Front? Just tell me, Ma - why do you hate Colonel Vye so much? What harm has he ever done to you?'

It was a question I'd asked myself from time to time in the past, but never more urgently than now. And then suddenly the answer came to me. Perhaps I read it in my mother's eyes. Something she had said weeks ago suddenly echoed in my head, '... fond of a young gentleman, one of the gentry'. At last I understood.

'It's your friend, isn't it? What was her name? Iris, that's it. The girl who had a baby and died in the workhouse.' Of course! Why hadn't I realised before? 'Colonel Vye was the child's father, wasn't he?'

Ma didn't need to speak; I knew from her face that I'd hit on the truth. 'Oh, heavens,' I said, 'that was a long time ago. Hasn't he made up for it now?'

'You can never make up for wickedness like that.' She glared at me for even daring to suggest such a thing. 'If you'd seen the state she was in, her poor heart broken and left to die alone in that awful place, while Rory Vye went on his own sweet way as though he hadn't a care in the world ... Well, you'd hate him too, just as much as I do.'

'For Tom's sake, though, can't you even thank him for what he's done to help us?'

'I don't know,' she said slowly. 'The words would probably stick in my throat, to be honest. I can't look at him without thinking of Iris. Let's see what Tom has to say, eh?' She grasped my hand. 'Now do you understand why I don't want you anywhere near a young man from that family? If the same thing should happen to you, it would kill me.'

'Philip's not like that.'

'You don't know what he's like. You might think you do but Iris probably thought she knew Master Rory, too, and look what happened to her. That boy's trouble, Grace. Leave him well alone.'

Ma had no need to worry about Philip, because he'd be off to France before long, and anyway, all I could think about was Tom. Just to see him again, and talk to him! We could make everything all right, I was sure of it, once he was safe home. There was no way of knowing exactly when he'd be arriving, so Ma went home at dinner time the next day to wait. I ran down to the gate lodge early that evening, only to discover that my brother was back, but fast asleep upstairs.

'How is he?' I asked my mother. 'Did he tell you what happened?'

'Not really. He seems very quiet.' The sink was full of wet clothes, which she went back to pounding against a washboard. 'Ugh! You should have seen the state of this uniform - it was crawling with lice. I've had to boil it and burn his underclothes; they'd have fallen apart in the wash.'

'But is he all right?' I persisted. 'Can I put my head round the bedroom door?'

'Leave him in peace for the minute. He needs

some time to himself.'

So I had to curb my impatience until the next morning. I found Tom sitting on his own in the front room, staring into space. 'Why, hello, Grace,' he said, looking faintly puzzled at the sight of me. He didn't make a move to get up.

I kissed him, and knelt by the chair. 'Tom! How are you? We've been so worried!'

'Oh, there's no need to worry about me. I'm all right. Right as rain.'

Of course he wasn't - anyone could see that. He'd had a wash and a shave, and dressed himself in a clean shirt and trousers, but he seemed completely at a loss as to what he was meant to do next. All the spirit that made him Tom seemed to have gone, and only the empty husk of a man with his face and body left behind. It was dreadful. I found myself yattering about nothing in particular - how wonderful it was to have him home, and all the things we could do over the next few days, and even that he'd be here for my birthday, which happened to be coming up - while all the time he gazed at me with that bemused expression, as if he couldn't quite remember who I was. After a little while, Ma came in.

'That's enough for now, Grace,' she said. 'You can come back this evening and we'll all have supper at home.'

'Oh, Ma,' I whispered in the kitchen, 'what's happened to him?'

'Give him time,' she said, but I could see she was just as worried. There wasn't a great deal of time left, for one thing. How could Tom go back to France in this state? We didn't even know for sure whether he'd be in the same company, or the same rank, and he seemed vague about that too. 'Stop badgering the poor lad,' Ma had told me sharply when I'd tried to ask. 'Don't you go upsetting him with all those questions.'

Supper was a little better. My father and I talked about the stables, and Tom seemed interested in the horses. 'Why don't you come up tomorrow?' Da suggested, laying down his knife and fork. 'We can put you to work.'

'See how you feel in the morning,' Ma said, beginning to clear away the plates. 'There's no rush.'

Tom must have been up with the lark, though, because he and my father came to open up the stables together the next morning, and he went with Da on a trip in the ambulance later on. Seeing men in a worse state than himself must have helped him, I think, because he began to look a little more like himself, although it was hard to say exactly how. He had his dinner with us, under the stag's head, and in the afternoon he and I polished the harness. We didn't need to talk; it was lovely just to be together and catch his eye to share a smile every so often. I felt as though he was thawing out; you could almost see it happen by the minute.

Father had to take out Lady Vye in the gig so we got Moonlight ready, and Tom seemed to enjoy that too. There's something so satisfying about brushing a horse: the feel of his muscles rippling under the warm, satiny coat, and the rhythmic sweep of your arm as you make your way around him, paying attention to the sensitive places where he'd like you to go gently. Moonlight's twitchy about his eyes, so I always work very light and quick around his face with a hay wisp, and chat to him while I'm doing it so he knows not to worry.

'Somebody's taught you well,' Tom said, and I realised he'd been standing back to watch me. 'I'd have you in my stables like a shot.'

We took Moonlight out to the yard and harnessed him up to the gig. Tom seemed to droop a bit after my father had driven it away, so I told him that there was no time to rest: we still had Daffodil to groom, and Bella too. He made an effort but his heart wasn't in it and after a little while, he went to sit down on a straw bale. I was about to make some joke about docking his wages, but then I saw his face and bit back the words.

'They don't run away, you know,' he said, folding the hair cloth into a tight little parcel.

'Who don't?' I asked, coming to sit beside him.

'Horses. They just stand there with the bombs raining down on them and wait to be killed. I suppose they don't realise what's happening, don't understand they can try to escape.' He let the cloth fall between his hands.

'What's it like over there?' I felt he wanted to tell me.

'Like nothing on earth. It's too awful, Grace - the things I've seen, the things I've had to do. You wouldn't want to know. But the funny thing is, it's the only place that seems real to me now. While I'm here with you, all safe and clean and comfortable, it feels as though I'm sleep-walking. I shall only come alive again when I'm back there, in the middle of hell. Yet how can I go back? I'm no use any more.'

'Oh, come on,' I said, trying to jolly him out of it. 'Of course you are.'

'No, I'm not. I've lost my nerve.' He looked at me again, agonised. 'Do you know what I did? I laid down my gun.'

That didn't sound so very bad to me - not bad enough to be shot for, anyway. 'What happened exactly?' I asked. 'Tell me about it. I'm sure it wasn't your fault.'

He laughed: a dry, mirthless sound. 'All right, I will, if you really want to know.' I noticed his hands were shaking, so I squeezed them between my own. They were deathly cold.

'We were on the Menin Road, just out of Ypres. Wipers, we call the place. Anyway, we'd been fighting to hold on to this crater for a while with the Huns shelling us all the time. Some fellows came along to relieve us at last, so we marched off, eight miles back to camp with our kit weighing us down. We were dead on our feet but they only let us sleep for two hours before we were woken up to get back there for a counter-attack, and nothing to eat or drink first except a mug of tea. So it was the same journey all over again, with a charge across open ground at the end of it. There were whizzbangs dropping everywhere and German snipers firing at us - the whole world was exploding. Suddenly there came an almighty blast and I thought the show was all over for me. Maybe I was unconscious for a while, I don't know. Anyway, I came to my senses eventually and crawled into a shell hole to wait for the racket to die down.

'I didn't see him at first, but somebody else had found the place before me. There was a Hun lying there, with his leg shot to pieces. We looked each other up and down, and I suppose we both decided this hidey hole was big enough to share. After a while, I thought I might as well patch him up a bit, so I did. Put a bandage over the wound, and gave him some water. He could speak a bit of English - better than my German, at any rate - and he thanked me very nicely for my trouble. He showed me a picture of his girl, and we shared a cigarette. I only had the one left. Funny, isn't it? We ended up sitting in that shell hole all night, and I felt quite fond of him by the morning. As soon as it became light enough to see, we shook hands and I found my way back to our trench. I knew the Huns would be sending out a party to collect their wounded, so he'd probably be all right.'

'Well, what was wrong with that?'

He laughed again. 'Everything. I should have killed Fritz or taken him prisoner, for a start, and I left my gun behind to make it ten times worse. "Shamefully casting away arms in the presence of the enemy," that's what they call it.'

'They found you innocent, though.'

'Only because of Colonel Vye. You should have heard the things he said about me, the statements he collected to prove I wasn't a coward. I hardly recognised myself! He told me later that he'd been to school with my commanding officer, which must have clinched it. In the end they decided I'd been concussed and couldn't be held responsible for my actions.' He shook his head. 'It's a game, Grace. Ordinary soldiers like me don't mean anything to the top brass. They expect us to be slaughtered without a murmur and don't give a damn about it until we stop killing in return. Well, I can't do it any more. I didn't forget my rifle: I left it behind on purpose because I won't ever fire it again. So you see, I'm a dud. No earthly use to anyone out there. Or over here, either, for that matter.'

I couldn't think of anything that would comfort him, so we just carried on sitting there for a while without speaking. And that was how Philip found us.

'Hello, old chap,' he said, holding out a hand for Tom to shake. 'I heard you were back. Thought maybe we could go for a ride together? Like the old times.'

Tom got up and they clapped each other hard on the back in the way I've noticed men seem to do when they're fond of each other. 'I should enjoy that,' Tom said - and I felt so relieved. Philip would know what to say.

Da came back to the stables not long after they'd left and told me to take myself off for a cup of tea, since Tom and I had been working so hard and got ahead of ourselves with the chores. I thought I'd see what Florrie was up to as we hadn't had a proper chat for a few days so, after a quick wash and brush-up, I made my way to the kitchen. Mr Fenton passed me in the corridor which was strange, as he was usually busy butlering upstairs at that time of day, but I didn't have a chance to wonder why. Someone had suddenly cried out from within the room. It was an unearthly noise, like nothing I had ever heard before: a single note of utter, heartbroken despair which turned my blood to water.

I knew instantly who was making that terrible sound, and why.

Chapter Sixteen

I have a strong feeling that I shall come through safely; but nevertheless, should it be God's holy will to call me away, I am quite prepared to go ... and you, dear Mother and Dad, will know that I died doing my duty to my God, my country, and my King ... Fondest love to all those I love so dearly, especially yourselves.

Your devoted and happy son, Jack

From a letter by Second Lieutenant John Engall to his parents from France, 1 July 1916. He was killed three days later, aged 20.

FLORRIE WAS SITTING THERE with Mrs Jeakes' arm around her shoulders and an open letter on the kitchen table in front of her. I recognised Alf's handwriting on the envelope from all the others she kept under her pillow, and for a moment, became foolishly hopeful. Perhaps it wasn't the very worst news? But Mrs Jeakes caught my eye and gave a little shake of her head.

'I'll put the kettle on,' she said quietly, getting up.

I took her place at the table and rubbed Florrie's back. She had begun to cry now: great gasping sobs that wracked her whole body. 'There, there, Florrie,' I murmured helplessly. All I could do was find a fresh handkerchief and put my arm around her, though I think she hardly knew I was there.

'Not my Alf,' she whispered when at last she could speak. 'Not my darling boy. How shall I manage without him?'

I had no idea. Alf was Florrie's whole world. She had no mother or father to love her, only solid, decent Alf Fortescue. Now he was dead, and all Florrie's dreams - a husband to cook for, a brood of fair-haired children who were the spit of him, a cottage with a garden for potatoes and runner beans - were gone too. Nothing I could say would take away the pain of that. I remembered what she'd once said to me, about standing at the edge of a cliff. Now she was falling, as she'd known she must, falling alone into an ocean of grief and likely to drown in it.

Eventually I helped her upstairs, to rest quietly by herself for a while. She'd put the letter in her pocket and at last I realised what it was: a note Alf had written to be sent only in the event of his death. Perhaps they'd sent the official telegram to his mother, if she was still down as next of kin.

I was making Florrie comfortable on the bed when she suddenly grasped my hand. 'At least we were married. No one can take my wedding day away from me. Alf knew I loved him, and I know he loved me - and I'll always have his ring. That's better than nothing, isn't it?'

Her words sent a pang into my heart, they were so brave and pathetic at one and the same time, but I managed not to cry and agreed that a wedding ring was more than many girls had to remember their sweethearts by. Then I went slowly downstairs, to tell my mother what had happened. What a deal of misery this war has brought into the world already! And who knows how much more there is to come

…

We go about our business very quietly and thoughtfully these days; Alf's death has cast a deeper shadow over this sad house. Lady Vye's told Florrie she can take a week's holiday, but there's nowhere for her to go. Swallowcliffe's the only home she has. 'Besides, I need to keep my mind occupied,' she tells Dora and me. 'At least work stops me thinking.'

It's been one shock after another since the news came of Lord Vye's death. The only good thing to hold on to now is the fact that Tom's sorted himself out. That's largely down to Philip, in my opinion. Tom has spent hours helping him on the wards after that first ride together, and it seems to have given him back a sense of purpose. The next thing we know, it's been arranged - with the help of Dr Hathaway and Colonel Vye - for my brother to be transferred from the artillery to the medical corps. He's to be a stretcher-bearer in the same hospital as Philip.

'I'm going to try and make a decent fist of this, Gracie,' Tom tells me when we're alone together for a moment. 'So long as I don't have to shoot at anybody, I think it will be all right. Besides, Philip will look out for me.'

'Look out for each other, won't you?' I ask, the voice catching in my throat and that dreadful knot of worry back in my stomach.

When will things ever be right again? I've been restless and uneasy all week, unable to settle to my work or sleep through the night without starting awake, worried to death about goodness knows what. It's as though a layer of skin has been peeled away; all my feelings are too close to the surface, liable to bubble up without warning. Whatever's the matter with me? Florrie's tears may be catching but life has been worse than this before and I've got through it without wanting to weep at the drop of a hat. I can't stop turning everything over in my mind: thinking, endlessly thinking. About Lord Vye and the man he's turned out to be; about his brother, the Colonel, and the debt of gratitude we owe him (my father's written a letter, although that's hardly enough for saving a man's life); about my mother, and the grievance she's nursed against Rory Vye for all these years; about Philip Hathaway, too.

One night, I wake up at dawn. It isn't worth trying to go back to sleep, even if by magic I could, for we'll have to be up in a couple of hours. So rather than lie there, tossing and turning in the stuffy room, I feel for a shawl and creep out to find a breath of air up on the roof. Light is stealing over the countryside, and with every passing minute the patchwork of fields and hedgerows is revealed more clearly as I stand there, leaning against a chimney stack. The bricks feel solid and warm at my back, even though the sun isn't up yet, and I rub against them to scratch it, like Daffodil under the oak trees. How quiet and lovely the world looks! And yet the sight of it brings me no peace.

For some reason I find myself thinking about my mother's friend, Iris, and once a picture of her has floated into my head, there's no room for anything else. Beautiful, doomed Iris, with hair yellow as butter, who died in the workhouse - along with her baby, no doubt. Did Colonel Vye know he'd fathered a child? He must have done; it would have been the only likely reason for Iris to have left the Hall so suddenly. And he did nothing for her? Just left her there to die, alone and abandoned? Maybe Ma has reason to hate him after all. If anyone treated a friend of mine like that - Florrie, or Daisy, or even Dora - I should find it hard to forgive them too.

And yet ...

And yet, the story doesn't ring true.

Philip's told me something about Colonel Vye which I know to be the case. 'He's always been keen on fair play,' that's what he said, and I realise in an instant the Colonel would never behave in such a way, even as a young man. How could I ever have thought so? He isn't the type to seduce a girl and abandon her without a backward glance. Somebody else in the family was, though. Daisy's voice cuts through the clamour in my head, ringing out clear as a bell. 'He was on the prowl - looking for some simple girl whose head would be turned by a few sweet words in a cut-glass accent.'

The truth is staring me in the face. Now I know who fathered Iris's baby, and it isn't Rory Vye.

It's hard to concentrate on my work in the morning (can it really be only yesterday?) and Da has to scold me a couple of times for carelessness. Luckily we both have the afternoon off, since Ma has arranged a treat for us to say goodbye to Tom, who's going back to France first thing today. She's made a picnic and we take a train down to the coast at dinnertime: the whole family, apart from Ivy. Lady Vye says Swallowcliffe will have to manage without the Stanburys for one afternoon, which is very decent of her.

It's lovely down by the sea. A bit nippy, with the sun hiding all morning and a breeze whipping up the water into frothy waves, but fresh and salty clean. There are some soldiers marching along the beach on exercises, but when they're out of sight, you can almost forget about the war. Of course we're sad because of Tom going off again, but he's so much better than he was that we're thankful for small mercies and trying to hope for the best. At least he won't have to carry a rifle. We find a sheltered spot and spread out our picnic: sandwiches, pork pies, crunchy red radishes from the garden, lemonade and ginger beer. Afterwards, Da and Tom play cards and Hannah drops off to sleep on the rug; the Vyes' baby is wakeful and she's disturbed most nights.

I want to get Ma on her own, so I take her off for a walk along the shingle, arm in arm. Every so often we can hear a dull thud and eventually we realise what it is: the sound of the guns in France, floating across the Channel. 'Poor souls,' Ma says, biting her lip. It's strange to hear noises from this other world, so very different from our own and yet not so far away.

Yet as you might imagine, for once I have other things on my mind than the war. There's no easy way of bringing up the topic so I just come out with it, fair and square. 'Ma, you know your friend Iris, who ended up in the workhouse?' She looks rather taken aback, but I plough on. 'Well, did she *tell* you that Colonel Vye was her baby's father?'

After a second or two, she gives me an answer. 'Not in so many words. It was clear enough, though, for anyone with an eye to see. If you'd watched him with her, Grace, you'd have known. He was such a flirt and she fell for it - hook, line and sinker.' She pauses, gazing out over the water. 'Iris told me she was involved with a gentleman. Who else could it have been? I saw him waiting for her in the boathouse one night.'

'Did you see his face? Are you absolutely certain it was him?'

'Yes, I am. Positive,' she replies (although just

for a second, is there the briefest flash of doubt in her eyes?). 'Look, I can understand why you don't want to accept what that man did after the way he's helped Tom. Perhaps he is a better person now, but I'll bet it's only because he feels guilty - and so he should. He was the one who did for Iris, I'd stake my life on it.'

There's nothing I can say to that, not having any definite proof, so I hold my tongue for the time being. I'm determined not to let the matter rest, though; it's as if I've made a pact with Iris to find out the truth. Why, I can't say. I feel she wants me to, that's all - which is ridiculous since we've never met and she must have died ten years before I was born, but there you are.

I think about the tricky matter of proof for the rest of that afternoon on the beach, and the walk back to the railway station, and the clackety-clack train journey to Edenvale, and the hansom cab ride back to Swallowcliffe since we're all tired and in the mood to treat ourselves. We have mutton chops for supper, and after that I forget about Iris for once because it's time to say goodbye to Tom; I have to be back at the Hall by ten and he's leaving early the next morning. Another dreadful, sad farewell - they don't get any easier with practice. I can't help wondering how Mrs Hathaway must be feeling, what with her husband and Philip both going off this time.

I don't sleep much better through the night,

but at least an idea comes to me in the wakeful early hours of this morning. There's one person who's been at the Hall with my mother for donkey's years and probably knew Iris too: Mrs Jeakes. Maybe she can tell me something useful? So I fairly race around the stables to get ahead of my chores and then slip away to the kitchen at eleven or so, when Da's taking Mrs Hathaway out in the dog-cart. I change into a skirt and wash my hands, but it's only halfway there that it occurs to me to wonder how I'll bring the subject up - or any subject at all, for that matter. There's no reason whatsoever for me to be in the kitchen.

Eventually I hit on the idea of running an errand and take a detour to the walled garden, where I spot one of the village lads dawdling about in the soft fruit cage.

'Cook's been shouting for these raspberries a good hour,' I say, snatching the basket out of his hands. 'If I don't take them straight away, you'll be in a whole heap of trouble.'

Mrs Jeakes isn't overjoyed at the sight of the raspberries. 'Put them on the table,' she says with a jerk of her head. 'Though why that daft gardener should be bothering us with dribs and drabs of fruit at odd times of the day is beyond me. Well, off you go. What are you fidgeting about for?'

'Ma'am, I'm trying to find something out,' I say in a rush. 'My mother's told me about a great friend she had years ago here at the Hall, who died sadly, and I was wondering where she was buried. Her name was Iris Baker. You didn't know her, did you, or know her family by any chance?'

Mrs Jeakes looks at me as though I'm mad. 'I'll say one thing for you, Miss Stanbury, you keep us all on our toes. There's no telling what tomfoolery you'll come up with next. Why should I know where this Iris was buried if your mother doesn't and they were such good friends? Back to the stables with you, and try to think about something useful for a change.'

'Please, Mrs Jeakes, I do so want to find out!'

'And I do so want to get on with my work. Now out of my sight this minute before I set you to skinning eels!'

I've almost reached the door before she calls out, 'Iris Baker worked in the still room and left in a hurry for the usual reason, I suppose. That's about all I know. Oh, and there's her recipe for rose-petal jam in the black book.'

'Thank you, ma'am.' That's better than nothing; at least I have a faint trail to follow. And if there's any trace of Iris Baker left in the still room after all these years, you can trust Bess to have sniffed it out. I decide to ask for a look at the black book first: a thick volume which lives in the still-room dresser, its leather binding cracked and pages splattered with ancient fruit stains.

'I want to make the rose-petal jam for my mother,' I tell Bess, looking over my shoulder to make sure Ma's nowhere near about (for the still room is next door to the housekeeper's parlour). 'It's a surprise, so don't say anything, will you?'

'I can find that one for you,' she says, licking a finger and thumb before flicking over the pages. I want to tell her to take more care: she's handling a precious relic. 'Here we are. I knew it was somewhere near the beginning.' Bess cracks the book's spine open to make the pages lie flat before passing it to me. 'Make sure you use the dark-red petals with a strong scent, and ask Mr McKinley first or he'll have your guts for garters. Don't come running to me for help, either, when it all goes wrong. I've heard about your efforts at marmalade from Dora.'

I let Bess run on and smooth my fingers over the paper, staring at Iris's faded handwriting as though it will bring her alive. She has an elegant copperplate script, very regular and even, beautifully laid out in the centre of the page. Proof the recipe's hers comes in the shape of two small initials, 'IB', written at the end of it; the bottom loop of the 'B' curved around the 'I' so that the two letters twine together in a shape of their own.

'You don't have to learn the thing by heart,' Bess says quizzically. 'Sit down here and copy it out.' She rummages for a pencil stub in a drawer, then slaps it down on the table with a strip of paper.

'Now I must run, there's a million and one things to do before dinner. *You* might have hours to moon over a recipe but not all of us are so lucky.'

'Wait, Bess. Before you go, just tell me - do you know anything about Iris Baker? She was the still-room maid here ... oh, it must have been twenty-five years ago.' That was when Ma first came to the Hall, wasn't it? 'She wrote out this recipe for rose-petal jam.'

'Never heard of her,' Bess snaps. 'Now don't take an age, and shut the door after you.'

Just my luck, I think when she's left, to corner Bess at the one moment she's too busy to talk and ask her about the one person at Swallowcliffe she doesn't know. I leaf through the book, holding it up to my face to smell the paper. Where are you, Iris? Why are you so hard to find? I take hold of the front and back covers and shake them. A tiny scrap of something dark flutters down from between the pages: it turns out to be a pressed violet, but anyone could have put the flower there, not necessarily her. Then my fingers detect something unusual. The coloured endpapers stuck to the book's back cover bulge a little. They are thicker than those at the front, unevenly thicker. Something is lying between them and the black leather binding.

My fingers trembling, I try to pry the endpaper loose. It doesn't come. I don't want to tear it so I look around for a knife or anything else that's sharp.

Nothing. One of my hair pins will have to do. I make a tiny hole, work the pin under the paper and seesaw it back and forth. And then at last I can peel the paper away, to reveal the corner of a photograph. With a little more careful work, I manage to pull it out ... and know immediately that I'm looking at Iris. She's standing in the still room, before the dresser in front of me now, exactly as I pictured her. She has thick fair hair escaping beneath her cap, dazzling skin that shines out of the picture as though it's lit up from inside, and she's smiling so happily it brings tears to my eyes. There's a date on the back of the photograph: 'March 1890' - written, I'm sure, by Iris herself.

Now I have her.

I have him, too. There's a second photograph slipped behind the endpaper. It shows Iris wearing what looks like a silk ballgown with white kid gloves up the elbow, and there's a message in another hand on the back. 'My love for ever, dearest. EV'.

EV. Edward Vye. Or as Daisy says, 'His Precious Lordship'.

I don't know how long I've been sitting here in the stables. The photographs are safely in an envelope, tucked away on the shelf among last year's feed receipts where no one will ever find them. They're too upsetting to look at any more. It's one thing to come up with a theory, no matter how strongly you might believe it, and another to hold the evidence right there in your hand. My thoughts run around in a circle, and this is where they keep ending up: Ma is wrong. She's hated Rory Vye and worshipped his brother for years, all because of a stupid mistake. And if she's wrong about one thing, she can be wrong about another.

You see, there's something I haven't told anyone. It hurts to admit how much I care for Philip Hathaway. Looking back, I probably fell in love with him that moment I opened my eyes in the wood and saw him sitting against the tree, watching me. He's honest and clever and kind, and the worst of it is, he might have loved me once, too. I've thrown all that away, because I listened to my mother and wasn't brave enough to stand up for myself. Now it's too late. He's gone to France and he probably won't come back; I shall never be able to tell him how I feel. That's really why Florrie's words had such an effect on me the other day. 'Alf knew I loved him, and I know he loved me.' She seized her chance of happiness with both hands, while I've let mine slip through my fingers.

I shall go mad if I sit here much longer, so I get up and fetch brushes from the harness-room. It's better to be busy, and I suddenly yearn to be with the horses. Daffodil could do with grooming and that will comfort me; she's so calm and wise somehow. I find myself talking to her as I work. She nuzzles me occasionally with her soft nose as though she's trying to cheer me up, so I start telling *her* how I feel about Philip, since I can't talk to anyone else. I tell her everything, even thoughts I can't remember having had before - how handsome he is, and how brave, and the way my heart pounded when he held me that time in the stable yard, and how much I hate Lydia Lovell - and she nods her head up and down occasionally as though she understands. 'Oh, Daffodil,' I sigh, laying my head against her neck, 'what am I going to do with myself now he's gone?'

Then I hear it. The tiniest noise, as though a mouse has scurried across the floor. It makes me whirl around with my heart in my mouth and my cheeks flaming red. Has someone been eavesdropping?

He's standing there. Philip himself. How can he be?

'What are you doing here?' I stammer. 'Why aren't you on the way to France?'

How much has he heard? I can't bear to imagine, I only want to die, for the ground to open and swallow me up, because I can tell from the way he's smiling that he must have been listening to me for some time.

'Mother's driving Father and me straight down to Dover this evening.' He doesn't take his eyes off my face. Then he says, 'Oh, Grace,' and holds out his arms.

Just that, 'Oh, Grace,' but the way he says it lets me know everything's going to be all right, and I go to him. There's no awkwardness or embarrassment any more, only a wonderful feeling of contentment, as though I've come home after a long journey. He kisses me, and I can feel my heart soaring up to heaven like a swallow wheeling across the sky. Whatever happens in the future, we shall always have this moment. No one can ever take it away.

THE END

About the Author:

Jennie Walters has had over twenty books published for children and teens, including the popular Party Girls series. She was partly inspired to write the 'Swallowcliffe Hall' stories by visits to beautiful old English country houses, including Kingston Lacey in Dorset, Belton House in Lincolnshire and Castle Howard in Yorkshire. When younger, she spent two years in a cliff-top boarding school converted from a Victorian mansion with wood-panelled rooms, a huge marble staircase and one of the largest collections of stuffed birds in England. Finding a silver housekeeper's châtelaine while clearing out her father-in-law's flat whetted her interest in Victorian servants and their masters and mistresses, and prompted her to create a fictional country house of her own.

Jennie lives in London with her husband and a dog, and has two grown-up sons.

For a fascinating insight into the world of English country houses and the families and servants who live in them, visit Jennie's website, packed with original photographs, historical information, extracts from servants' letters, and much more!

www.jenniewalters.com

Other books in the Swallowcliffe Hall series:

Isobel's Story, 1939

Isobel comes to Swallowcliffe Hall in 1939, to stay with her grandmother Polly. She's meant to be resting after a serious illness, but talk of war is on everyone's lips and it's an anxious time – especially for Andreas, a Jewish boy who has managed to escape from Germany on the Kindertransporte. Can Izzie possibly help his family find sanctuary at the Hall too? She is determined to try, although the house has fallen on hard times and its very existence is threatened. Attempting to heal old wounds, she uncovers a family secret that has remained hidden for years, and discovers courage in the face of danger and prejudice she never knew she had.

'This historical novel is full of excitement and adventure and I couldn't put it down, I would recommend it to anyone.' *An Amazon customer*

And for a look at life in Swallowcliffe Hall from the other side of the green baize door:

Eugenie's Story, 1893

This is the journal of Eugenie Vye: the prettiest debutante of the 1890 season, with hair she can sit on and a seventeen-inch waist – yet somehow three years later, still unmarried. Lord Vye's daughter might be thought to want for nothing, but life isn't easy on fifty guineas a year with a jealous stepmother watching one's every move. Eugenie's passionate nature and unerring ability to get hold of the wrong end of the stick land her in trouble as she follows her heart: from elegant Swallowcliffe to the streets of fashionable London, by way of rural Ireland, glamorous *belle époque* Paris and an idyllic artists' retreat at Giverny. She hurtles from one near-disaster to another, rescued only by a sense of humour, unquenchable optimism and her dear American friend Julia – until finally discovering love was right under her nose all along.

Printed in Poland
by Amazon Fulfillment
Poland Sp. z o.o., Wrocław